PENGUIN BOOKS
A FUNNY THING HAPPENED ON THE WAY TO THE CEMETERY

Carl Muller completed his education from the Royal College,
Colombo, and has served in the Royal Ceylon Navy and Ceylon
Army. In 1959 he entered the Colombo Port Commission and
subsequently worked in advertising and travel firms. Muller took
up journalism and writing in the early Sixties and has worked in
leading newspapers in Sri Lanka and the Middle East. His
published works in Sri Lanka include *Sri Lanka—a Lyric*, and *Father
Saman and the Devil* as well as a link language reader for students,
*Ranjit Discovers where Kandy Began*. *The Jam Fruit Tree*, the first part
of the Burgher trilogy, was published by Penguin in 1993 and was
awarded the Gratiaen Memorial Prize for the best work of English
Literature by a Sri Lankan for 1993, a prize endowed by Booker
Prize winning international author Michael Ondaatje. The two
sequels to *The Jam Fruit Tree*, *Yakada Yakā* and *Once Upon a Tender
Time*, were published by Penguin in 1994 and 1995 respectively.
*Colombo—A Novel* was published by Penguin in 1995. A Puffin titled
*The Python of Pura Malai and other Stories* was published in early
1995.

Carl Muller lives in Kandy, the hill capital of Sri Lanka, with his
wife and four children.

PENGUIN BOOKS
A MONKEY TIME LED ON THE WAY TO THE CEMETERY

Carl Muller completed his education from the Royal College Colombo and has served in the Royal Navy and Ceylon Army. In 1959 he entered the Colombo Port Commission and subsequently worked in advertising and travel firms. Muller took up journalism and writing in the early Sixties and he worked in leading newspapers in Sri Lanka and the Middle East. His published works in Sri Lanka include Sri Lanka—a Lyric, and Father Saman and the Devil as well as a stage-language adaptation from Valmiki's celebrated epic. The first of the trilogy, the first part of the Burgher trilogy, was published by Penguin in 1993 and was awarded the Gratiaen Memorial Prize for the best work of English Literature by a Sri Lankan, for 1993. A prize endowed by Booker Prize winning international author Michael Ondaatje. The two sequels to The Jam Fruit Tree, Yakada Yaka and Once Upon a Tender Time were published by Penguin in 1994 and 1995 respectively. Colombo, A Novel was published by Penguin in 1995. A further titled The Children of Poor Mano and other stories was published in early 1995.

Carl Muller lives in Kandy in full enjoyment of Ceylon, with his wife and four children.

# Carl Muller

# A FUNNY THING HAPPENED ON THE WAY TO THE CEMETERY

PENGUIN BOOKS

Penguin Books India (P) Ltd., 11 Community Centre, Panchsheel Park,
New Delhi 110 017, India
Penguin Books Ltd., 27 Wrights Lane, London W8 5TZ, UK
Penguin Putnam Inc., 375 Hudson Street, New York, NY 10014, USA
Penguin Books Australia Ltd., Ringwood, Victoria, Australia
Penguin Books Canada Ltd., 10 Alcorn Avenue, Suite 300, Toronto,
Ontario M4V 3B2, Canada
Penguin Books (NZ) Ltd., Cnr Rosedale and Airborne Roads, Albany, Auckland,
New Zealand

First published by Penguin Books India (P) Ltd. 1995

10  9  8  7  6  5  4

Typeset in New Baskerville by Digital Technologies and Printing Solutions,
New Delhi

This book is, as the author claims, a work of 'faction' and, while fixed both
historically and chronologically, remains fiction, based on fact, embroidered
and distorted in order to protect the characters herein. All names, save where
obviously genuine, are fictitious and any resemblance to persons living or dead
is wholly coincidental.

Printed at Basu Mudran, Calcutta

*'A little measly talk over neighbours is right enough; it do make the day go by a little quicker and sends a body to bed with a chuckle'*

Mrs Ellis's VILLAGER

# *Contents*

Foreword                                              ix

Here Comes The Queen!                                  1
The Old Folks At Home                                 11
This Demi-Eden . . .                                  21
You Scratch My Back . . .                             31
That Dread Bread Spread                               41
The Python Of Pura Malai                              47
Confucius He Say . . .                                63
Go, Man, Go!                                          75
God Equals Claud                                      83
Oh The Manners . . . Oh The Customs                   99
Seventy Millimetres Of Trouble                       107
The Unhinging Of Hillocks                            117
The New God Of The Gulf                              129
Rub-A-Dub-Dub                                        139
Ups And Downs                                        153
With Flying Colours                                  161
Guide Me, I'm A Tourist                              171
A Crack At The Mirror                                179
Comply And Complain                                  193

# Foreword

A friend with a gloomy disposition once remarked that we are all, from the day we are born, dying. We are all on the way to the cemetery. He took great satisfaction in this pronouncement, thinking, doubtless that it was quite a cheering observation. The philosophy of the fatalist, to be sure, but who would deny the truth of it. Natural optimism tells me to perish the thought. My own road to the cemetery has been tolerably long and, who knows, it may end at the next bend. It is time to put down a few things—those funny things that have happened on the way to the cemetery. Let they who wish to write my epitaph put it in three words: 'He died laughing!'

# Foreword

# Here Comes The Queen!

> A cat may look upon a queen, I think,
> But can a sailor tip the queen a wink?

In 1953 I joined the Royal Ceylon Navy. It was the eighteenth of November and not the sort of day to be looked kindly upon. Once signed on, I was asked to swear allegiance to Her Majesty the Queen of England and was then kitted out in duck cap and whites. With the rest of the recruit intake, I was then drafted—yes, that's the word—to H.M.Cy.S. Rangalla, a training establishment four thousand feet up in Sri Lanka's central mountains. That's where the bracing weather made everything nip and tuck and even old ladies were assessed for whatever tattered potential remained. The sea had to be imagined. A nice way to begin life as a sailor!

It was believed, by bow-legged naval types who strutted decks, that it takes about three months of torrid damns and blasts and what-the-fucks to make the average civilian into a below par sailor. That's what's done, it was said, in Portsmouth and Plymouth and other places of nautical suffering; and the Royal Ceylon Navy was modelled and moved quite clodhopperly on Royal Navy lines. There was no other way.

Training went on apace and then, in the final month came a signal from Naval Headquarters in Colombo which plunged the camp into disarray. Her Majesty, Queen Elizabeth II of England, it said quite breathlessly, would visit Sri Lanka. Would it please the Commanding Officer of Her Majesty's training vessel Rangalla to drill his recruits until he was blue in the face so that said recruits were shipshape and seaworthy enough to be the Queen's Royal Guard of Honour.

The more naïve among us considered this honour indeed, but it was later revealed that this was a matter of simple naval expediency. Recruits, we were informed by a worldly-wise Leading Seaman, were in possession of new uniforms and were thus better equipped to uphold the prestige of the force before a visiting sovereign. Q.E.D.

All other routine was dumped. Life became an endless round of marching, marching, forming rank and presenting arms. A Guards Instructor of the Royal Navy named Brady came to Rangalla to look us over and blew several fuses. His broad Yorkshire accent made him quite unintelligible to the main body of those he had come to persecute. This made for rather bizarre and quite unreal moments when he waddled up to take command.

'Roy . . . yell grrrth! Ain . . . heh!'

We stared at him nonplussed.

Brady turned to the Platoon Commander with the sort of concern one usually feels after a hurricane warning. 'Dahn't these mehn know their drill aht ahll?'

The platoon commander was a most impatient man. Also, he didn't like this stuffy G.I. from Blighty very much. 'Oh, they know their stuff,' he assured. 'Let me handle 'em.'

He swung on us murderously. 'Royal Garrrrdd! Hough! Stand still! Don't move a frothing eyelid! Slooooop arrmz! Head erect! Simmons! Is your mother a bloody Kathak dancer? Now the queen steps onto the saluting dais . . . Roooy'l Gaarrrd . . . Royal Saloooot . . . Prezent arrrms! Slap those rifle butts sharply! Smartly! My

God, Fernando, I'll kick you all the way up Fox Hill!'

G.I. Brady looked as though he had just been forcefed with the square of minus x.

'Well, G.I., that's the way to get things done around here.'

'Ayh . . . very good, sir. Only the Quain meh not—ah-approve.'

'Don't give it a thought. She doesn't know these buggers.' He turned on us. 'Sloo000 . . . arrmz! Orderr arrmz! Now listen. The Queen will inspect you. She will walk past you accompanied by the Royal Guard Commander and Prince Phillip and the Commanding Officer of the Guard. Now G.I. Brady will be the Queen and I am the Royal Guard Commander.' He led Brady to a far corner of the parade ground. 'Look lively there!' he yelled. 'Here comes the Queen!'

This was too much. Someone muttered, 'Just look at them. Two bloody lunatics!'

The Platoon Commander waltzed up, hand holding an imaginary sword. Behind him minced Queen Rosie O'Brady the First and the Last. The Royal Guard tittered. 'Daft' Fernando tried to suppress an insane giggle and went 'woof', and roars of laughter split the morning air.

The Platoon Commander lost his last shreds of dignity.

'Stop it!' he foamed. 'Stop laughing!'

We hooted. Sick Bay attendant Winnie went into convulsions of a sort and had to be thumped vigorously. Simmons pointed helplessly at Brady. 'Here comes the Queen,' he howled, and the eruptions of laughter scared the crows off the yardarm.

'High port arms!' the Platoon Commander screeched, doing a sort of Watusi. 'High port arms! Run, you bastards, run! Run!'

We ran . . . round and round the parade ground for a very long time. We lost touch with time as well as space. There wasn't a laugh left in any of us when we were finally brought to a tottering halt. Of G.I. Brady there was nary a sign.

A week later we were herded into ten ton trucks and driven at breakneck speed down the mountains. G.I. Brady would continue to train us in Colombo, in the headquarters shore establishment H.M.Cy.S. Gemunu.

At the gates of Gemunu we were mustered and looked over by a frosty bloke with pimples. 'From now on consider yourselves the royal welcome service,' he said coldly. 'After colours every morning you will fall in for parade. Number ten drill order. I don't have to warn you about your turnout. We have more imagination than the chaps at Rangalla and use it better . . .'

Every morning thereafter, Brady had us in his tender care. His was the determination to do or die for his Queen. We marched. God, how we marched. We were even marched along the streets of Colombo in ceremonial number six uniform. We saluted the Queen so many times a day that the poor lady must have had queasy afternoons and incredibly dreamy nights. We practiced street lining and were scattered all over city roads where stray dogs sniffed at our boots and lifted hind legs eagerly.

'Muller! Your rifle is ten degrees out. Keep that fucking forearm parallel to the ground!'

'It's parallel sir.'

'It's not! Don't argue!'

I shifted my elbow a fraction.

'Simmons, your web belt is a disgrace! And there's brass polish on the canvas!'

Simmons kept mum. Nothing helped when the Guard Commander was on the prod. Unless it was a big orang-utan walking along the road singing 'Swanee'.

'Fernando! Fall out. Fall out! What is that thing on your head?'

'My cap sir.'

It was his cap, naturally, but he did not regale us with the interesting story of how it flew off his head when he was on the flag deck of the signal tower and how it was thereupon flattened by a passing jeep on the road below.

'You call that a cap? That's like a fucking urinal! Are you going to stand on the quay with a cap like that? Do you want to disgrace the Royal Guard?'

As the days sped by, this business of disgrace became more profound, vast in scope. We were, it seemed, reaching for the Ultimate State of Abjection. 'Do you want to disgrace the Navy . . . your country . . . your father and mother . . . me?' By the time the full dress rehearsal on the quay came around, we had smeared and sullied the good name of everything within and beyond reach—the South East Asia region, the Commonwealth of Nations, the East Indies Fleet, the Captain of the Navy . . .

Having displayed our firm intentions to wallow in sinks of undrilled iniquity, we were by no means disposed to having the Queen think unkindly of us. We brought forth reserves of elbow grease in order to present, at the fateful hour, a brave show. Prince Phillip, we were informed, would wear the uniform of the Admiral of the Fleet. Well, we would be as good a part of the fleet as any!

'She's quite a peach, isn't she?'

'Who?'

'The queen.'

'Wha—oh, yes. Good looker. Nice legs too.'

'You know,' I mused, 'I wonder what'll happen if one of us tips her a wink.'

'Good God,' breathed Stoker Mechanic Ronald Todd.

'I say,' someone sang out, 'pukka idea!'

'So what's a wink,' another said, 'Comes and goes—*phut!* like a flash, no?'

The idea festered. 'So what'll she do? She's a queen, no? She's got to queen it.'

Some gaped. Others chuckled. 'So OK,' I said (and it wasn't after canteen beer either), 'if she looks at me I'll just shut one eye . . . very slowly.'

Whoops of laughter, but barely an hour later the bosun's pipe screeched. 'Royal Guard will fall in outside the quartermaster's lobby.' Hell, was the queen making a premature appearance?

'All right! Who's the bastard who's going to wink at the queen?'

So the cat was out and ranging free. A tattle-tale in the mess.

'Just having fun, sir. Just thinking, the queen is a knockout, isn't she . . .'

'So you will wink at her?'

'But the sun may get in my eyes, sir . . .'

'I see . . . ' very sweetly, then: 'Do you want to cause a bloody international incident! You in this habit of winking at any bloody woman you see? So that's the type of bugger you are?'

'But, sir, no harm in winking at a pretty girl . . . .'

'Oh izzatso? Well, let me tell you something, you—you—lecher! When you are in the Queen's uniform you will not wink at girls! You will respect and honour your uniform! Is that clear!!'

'Yes, sir.'

'Good. I don't suppose you will actually have the balls to wink at the Queen but I've heard a lot about you. All of you! You are the worst intake of recruits we ever had the misfortune to select. We are still getting reports about

8

you from Rangalla as well as from the Army and Air Force camps there. So!' very fiercely. 'You were a pain in the arse there but you're not going to be a pain in the arse here! This is a disciplined fighting force. Not a bloody home for vagrants! And,' glaring at me, 'sex maniacs!'

He eyeballed us fiercely. His hands clenched and unclenched in the way the Boston strangler's would. 'Muller! I'll be watching you! Like a bloody hawk! If you bat an eyelid, so help me . . . bloody lunatics! Wink at the Queen! Get out! Get out! Dismissed!!'

We were very glad to.

There was a bit of a mish-mash on the following day. Lined up on the quay with the royal yacht *Britannia* tied up alongside, we awaited the Queen of England. We had marched out of camp, band leading—to the pier where we were inspected by G. I. Brady, the Captain of the Navy and cohorts of officers. The morning sun set our ceremonial bayonets ablaze and gilded the brass on our webbing. We looked good—and we knew we looked good.

First out of the royal yacht, stepping daintily in a dress of cool apple green, was the Queen's lady-in-waiting. Perhaps she jumped the gun, but on sighting her the Navy jumped the gun too. A 21-gun salute from the Galle Buck battery pounded the air with great hollow thumps, like a giant smacking his Wellingtons for reasons best known to himself. *Bwackh! Bwackh! Bwackh!* It was only after the Ceylon Armoured Corps had ceased firing that it was realized that an enthusiastic island had accorded the Queen's lady-in-waiting a royal salute, doubtless raising her self-esteem several notches. Later, the Army maintained that the Navy had given the signal to fire and there was much recrimination with lots of heavily-worded signals.

Her Majesty Queen Elizabeth II stepped onto the

saluting dais in perfect peace and quiet, punctured maybe by the querulous hoots of an uncaring tugboat. Then came the squeaky warble of a Lieutenant Commander telling us that we should, in a body, present arms. Prince Phillip saluted briskly. The Royal Standard clapped boisterously in the breeze. The band played 'God Save the Queen'. We stood as stiff as sticks of Brighton rock!

A pretty cursory inspection. An officer marched ahead and turned to face me, glaring balefully as the Royal party approached. The Queen ignored us both. There is no earthly reason why a reigning sovereign should look into any particular sailor's face, is there? As far as I know the only sailor's face she gazed earnestly into was Prince Phillip's . . . and she went and married him!

Well, Your Majesty, we've both come a long way since then. We have our grandchildren too. But, given the ghost of a chance you may have got a fat, juicy wink in 1954!

Call it a Third World tribute!

# *The Old Folks At Home*

> This business of rebirth is not so bad . . .
> But soft, that crocodile could be your dad!

I have to consider this convoluted business of rebirth.[*]
Nothing new, this business. We have so many
'born-again' Christians today that one wonders whether
this whole business of Original Sin is a flop. One grows
up, sows one's wild oats, cuts the mustard and lives it up.
Situations could become as sticky as last month's fondue.
Then whammo! One sees the light. Eyes roll
heavenwards, organ music with three flats billows, and one
is 'born again'.

By and large, we all accept in one way or another, by
dogma, precept or philosophy, that life as we know it is
finite. But, as demonstrated by the celebrated John Brown,
the soul keeps marching on. The sole trouble with Man,
then, is the soul trouble, and we insist—or, at least, the
dogma-wallahs do—that animals have no souls (just a
granny's knot at the base of the cortex) and are happily
in no need of eternal life insurance. So animals don't need
churches and ponderous priests. Man does.

In Sri Lanka, predominantly a Buddhist country,
rebirth is accepted as a matter of fact. One lives and dies
and it's back to the drawing board. What you become in
the next innings largely depends on how well you fared in

---

[*] The events of this story first appeared in *Yakada Yakā* (Penguin, 1994).

the first. If the cosmic moulders and modellers feel that you had it made in your previous incarnation but lacked such saving graces as humility, charity and sympathy for want and deprivation, you could be reborn a beggar. It's all part of the process of celestial education. The Buddhist takes this business all the way. If you don't watch your p's and q's this semester, you could be a boll weevil or a civet cat the next.

This puts paid to the Christian contention that animals are soulless. If one, in a long procession of lives, returns as a shipping moghul, a prize pig, a congenital idiot or a hippopotamus, the soul will continue to thread these many incarnations together; remain the common factor. Whatever the right-angled triangle, it will be the hypotenuse, and to the devil with Pythagoras! The general idea is that you mind how you treat that mangy cur in the gutter. It could be your great aunt Mathilda!

And all this preamble because of my father's table fan!

My father was an engine driver in the government railway and we lived for some time in Anuradhapura, an ancient capital of Sri Lanka which saw its heyday about 2500 years ago. On the upstairs balcony of our railway bungalow my father had a writing desk, a beat-up rattan chair and on the desk a large cowrie which served as a paper weight. He would sit here to write up his 'train tickets'—a sort of work log he needed to submit to the railway enginemen's office at the end of each work day. Stations were listed, times of arrival and departure, delays noted and reasons for such delays curtly explained; number of work hours calculated and, most important, the excess time done over the stipulated eight hours.

Sri Lanka is a small island. An engine driver stationed in Anuradhapura will take a train north or south, and whatever direction he points his engine in, he is expected to reach his final destination in six hours at the most. Oh, he has leeway: taking the engine in and out of the Locomotive Running Shed, coupling and uncoupling train, shutting down steam, all that sort of thing. Still, a normal eight hour shift was considered ample to do it all in, including the nitty gritty.

But Sri Lanka's engine drivers have ably demonstrated over the years, and to a long line of very frustrated railway efficiency experts, that the incurring of overtime was never an exception. Any and every day's work merited overtime and thus, extra wages. Trains have to be on time . . . the driver's time. Nothing could be simpler.

Hence the desk, the chair, the paper weight, and, since Anuradhapura in its balmiest of moments is infernally hot, a table fan on that desk to cool the brow in that fevered hour when a train ticket is in the making.

How the ratsnake came to the balcony is anyone's guess. It could have taken the stairs but my guess was that it simply heaved itself over the balcony rail via the wild olive tree whose branches tickled the house in many sensitive spots. The ratsnake's coming was not noted, nor was the order of its coming waited on.

We had just moved into Railway Town. Downstairs were scenes of domestic havoc as my mother and sisters put home into order. This is the time when left shoes go missing and someone places a dozen eggs on a bed and someone else sits on them and it is discovered that the curtains don't fit. The balcony was the eye of this domestic cyclone, and quick to realize this, my father had hung up his shingle there. There was no garden worth writing to the Prime Minister about. Lots of thorny, wild mimosa, big rain trees towering and glowering over a black iron rail fence, some very dejected oleander and a wild lime tree.

So it was that engine driver Vernon Muller sat at his desk, rubbed his hands together and stuck out a finger to switch on his fan. Pandemonium ensued. Sounds of a 200-pound male falling over, the dry-wood *brekk!* of a snapping rattan chair and above all, the roar, full of anger, fright, blue shock and the ignominy of the fall. There he sat, rubbing his hip amid the ruins of his chair, yelling wildly at a whopping big ratsnake curled lovingly around the fan. It seemed to enjoy this demonstration of human discomfiture. It gazed on my father with almost lazy interest, curled its tail disdainfully and said 'yah' by flicking a derisive tongue.

An upstairs balcony facing the road is a pretty public place. Passers-by could assess a tenant's status by what went on on his balcony. At the moment one such showed lively interest. He was a railway linesman who lived hard by. He nipped through our gate and began to semaphore frantically. Above the general hub-bub he was shrieking something about his grandmother.

'Get rid of that snake,' my father snarled, 'and what's that idiot yelling about?' He leaned over the rail. 'What the hell do you want?'

The man barged indoors, raced up the stairs. My mother, who was sure it had to be a marauder, seized a broom and raced behind. In her book marauders were dealt with with something long and heavy, hence the broom.

'Don't hurt her,' the man howled, 'that's my grandmother!'

This was quite unreal. We watched, fascinated, as the man went to the ratsnake, making littie cooing noises of conciliation. 'There, there, these people won't hurt you.

Where is grandfather? Why you leave him alone and come to here? Why you doing like this?' He stroked the snake's head lovingly and urged it to come along, there's a good girl. The creature uncoiled, slumped to the desk and poured itself onto the floor. 'That's right. You go home. Grandfather must be waiting, no?'

The ratsnake gave him a reproachful look. 'Nobody cares for old people,' it seemed to say, and swung off the rail to a wild olive branch. In a twinkling it disappeared in the foliage to appear an instant later at the base of the tree, then vanish.

'My grandmother,' the linesman said proudly, 'very sorry she disturb you.' Mother put up her broom with a sigh of regret.

'Cut that bloody branch,' Father said. 'No more visits from your relatives, do you hear!'

The linesman gave a pained nod. He said that long years ago his grandparents had lived in a hut right where our present bungalow stood. They had planted the olive tree. This time around, Grandpa and Grandma had been reborn as a pair of ratsnakes. Yes, they lived under the olive tree. In the garden he showed us the hole between the roots. He put a hand on my shoulder. 'They very nice. Even in last birth they very nice peoples. You look after them, no?'

I promised. Sharp barks of indignation still issued from the balcony: 'Look at my chair! Like a bloody jigsaw puzzle!'

Even as we spoke, Grandma (or was it Grandpa?) poked a head out and looked at us all-knowingly. Introductions were in order. 'This boy will bring and give eggs once in a way and milk. He is good boy. All good peoples here. Only don't go in the house, orl right?'

'They can eat all the rats and frogs here,' I offered,

and he beamed. Even the ratsnake's marbled look softened.

They were a handsome couple. Grandfather was the quieter, more sedate of the two. Regular pipe and slippers type. Grandmother was a bit of a gadabout. They would waft around the garden with lazy ease, regally accept the eggs I offered them each day (while neighbouring drivers and guards wondered why their hens laid less) and took to sunning themselves on our door rug. They liked to swing around the kitchen where a nervous cook would climb the hearth and sing arias until they went away. They became regular family pets. My little sister, Heather, just seven years old, would sit prattling to them, and they, Lord bless them, would appear to listen and nod and sway and curl around the potted palms.

One day only one of the pair appeared. It lay, half out of the hole, scorned an egg and gazed glassily and with that dejected air of a nun who had just been passed over by the Pope without a benign nod. I summoned the linesman. 'Aiyo,' he said, '*Seeya* must be sick!' (That's 'grandfather' in Sinhala). He asked grandmother what the trouble was and his face grew quite haggard. With adze and crowbar he began excavations. Grandpa lay dead inside, his body covered with ants. Sadly, he brought out the snake and asked for a box to take it away in.

'What about her?' I asked.

He shook a sad head. 'I don't know. Now she alone, poor lady.'

Poor lady. She mooned around like that knight-at-arms of the poem who was asked what ailed him. Even the neighbours came to pay their respects and offer condolences. A week later we found her at the foot of the olive tree. Dead. Our linesman took it pretty hard at first, then brightened up. 'They come back soon. They get reborn, no?' As what, he hadn't the foggiest.

Father thought deep and darkly about the prospect. Uncertainty smote him ham-fisted. He went to the balcony and stared morosely at the olive tree. Then he trotted off to the railway yard where he conscripted a couple of coolies. By evening the olive tree was no more. The sun would blaze fiercely on the balcony but that did not matter. Mother grumbled at the mess in the garden.

'Those old buggers planted the tree, no?' Father reasoned. 'So cut the bloody tree down and they won't come back!'

'How can you believe all that rubbish? In vain you cut that tree!'

'What if they come back? As bloody pythons? You want pythons on the balcony and under the beds?'

Then he stomped out to the Railway Institute to drown his sorrows. He always had so much that needed drowning . . . .

*This Demi-Eden . . .*

This Demi-Eden

How wonderful this island in the sun,
Where greedy, pliant boys are half the fun!

In the 1960s a headline in a German tourist rag caused a great deal of weeping and wailing and gnashing of teeth among officials of the Sri Lanka Tourist Board and the Department of Culture:

DO YOU WANT A BOY?
DO YOU WANT A GIRL?
SRI LANKA IS THE PLACE TO GO!

Sri Lanka's ambassador in Bonn made high squeaks of protest, but the rag was circulated around the offices of the Tourist Board and lots of red-faced officials walked around and rushed down corridors exclaiming 'did you ever?' and 'well I never!'

This was dashed embarrassing. How does a government inform tourist hotels and tour operators that they must pin down and discourage tourists who are sexually on the prod? Even Whitehall, I believe, would have balked. I mean to say, there's no official label, is there? A passport does not specify that Dieter Wasserman is an homosexual by occupation. Said Herr Wasserman is a respectable candle-maker from Stuttgart. He has lots of dollars and is on a thirty-day holiday. He is booked at the Hotel Lanka Oberoi, has accepted an impressive tour itinerary and placed himself in the hands of a reputed travel agency. His currency declaration form reveals that he has enough travellers cheques to plug the hole in the next national budget. Herr Wasserman is thus an honoured and most welcome visitor. Even the candles he manufactures are referred to with a sort of reverential awe. He is free to light his wick wherever he chooses!

Some people I believe—like the fabled Greeks—accept the rationale that in a storm, any port will do! The new permissiveness that rattled the moral foundations of society in the Sixties, saw the gays getting gayer, no longer trammelled by stricture and proud of their particular preferences. A sort of men's lib, actually, where heterosexual males turned away from mannish, impertinent women to seek solace with more pliant, understanding and amenable boys. It's not a new phenomenon, of course, but this business has stayed under wraps as long as society upheld the accepted yin-yang theory. Nobody wished to admit openly that more complicated permutations did exist; and its persistence became most confusing and downright abhorrent to those who had come to regard sex as traditionally decreed and quite a cut-and-dried business. It was most distressing to have simple, straightforward concepts shot full of holes!

As I write this, the doctor who is the Medical Director of the Sri Lanka Family Planning Association, has declared, indignantly, that homosexual foreigners flow like the Tiber in Sri Lanka. They swarm in 'in search of boys who are in plenty and very cheap.' She accused: 'The poverty-stricken youth, mainly in their teens, would do anything for a few rupees which a foreigner regards as throw-away money.'

But I now have a story to tell which will make the good

24

doctor and many other theorists sit up and wonder what hit them.

At some indeterminate time in my life which, may I remind, is shortening by the hour, I was a Tours Executive for a large Colombo travel firm. Came the day when a very rich German client arrived. He was a Count, no less, exuding dignity and wealth from every pore. He demanded a personalized service, an air-conditioned limousine, chauffeur and his own personal guide. The guide must also be fluent in German and was on no account to click his heels and say 'Sieg Heil.'

German-speaking guides were not easy to pin down in those days. Also, not the young, energetic fellow our client insisted on. But, after some frantic telephoning, a middle-aged, scholarly type was found who could say a sort of Teutonic Lord's Prayer and knew what Achtung meant. The men met in my office. German flowed like the Rhine in spate. Lots of Dankes and Bittes, gutturals galore. Like Louis Armstrong having strong words with an excavator. It was agreed that they would leave on tour immediately.

Two weeks later, they returned. A most successful expedition. High praise for the guide. Our client was deposited in a hotel and the guide returned to sort out expenses . . . and regale us with a wondrous tale.

They had taken the southern coastal route. Colombo to Galle and eastward-ho where the second evening was spent in the rest-house at Hambantota. (No, don't bother about a map, just revel in the action.)

The rest-house keeper at Hambantota was delighted. Place is a backwater at the best of times. A rich German tourist was manna from above. The German (who I shall call Himmler because of his taste for hims rather than hers) had performed well. He was a most considerate and

25

very cultured customer. The first night at the New Oriental Hotel, Galle, was quite perfect. He had seen the sights, dined elegantly, asked intelligent questions, evinced a keen interest in all he saw and tipped lavishly. Our guide was a happy man.

It was late afternoon when they reached Hambantota. A shower, change, and Himmler sat in the airy veranda, beer in hand, enjoying the seascape and the fuss of fishing boats bobbing into the bay. The rest-house keeper, after an initial kowtow and having got in everybody's way, stepped into the garden to supervise an old villager who had been conscripted to pluck coconuts.

Our guide was quick to draw Himmler's attention to the scene. There stood the old coconut plucker. He surveyed the tall palms and decided that the nuts on several were mature enough to be picked. To belly up a palm one needs the free use of arms and legs. The man reached down, took up the ends of his sarong and raised them skywards, then wrapped them diaper-fashion, firmly around his crotch. Regular old spindleshanks—wizened, gap-toothed, parading the green with his buttocks black as sin. His sarong had now become the skimpiest of lioncloths.

Himmler leaned forward with keen interest. The old man shinned up the first tree, knees splayed out, lean muscles tautening and rippling along his thighs. Himmler showed signs of a certain agitation. He rose and hopped into the garden and the guide skipped behind to drag him to safety as the coconuts began to bounce down. In a trice, the old man shimmied down, grinned hideously and strode to the next tree. Himmler watched, breathing hard. He turned to the guide. 'That man. I want. You tell him come to my room, hein?'

The guide was puzzled. 'You want to give him something?'

'Ach yes. Very fine man. You call him.'

The coconut plucker, whose name was Andiris and who was sixty-two years old, was summoned to the presence.

'This foreigner,' said the guide in the lingo, 'is very impressed at the way you pluck coconuts.'

Spindleshanks, with sarong still tucked jauntily between his legs, grinned and showed a mouthful of broken, betel-stained teeth. Close up he looked more repulsive than ever. He salaamed and asked for ten rupees.

'What did he say? What did he say?' asked Himmler.

'He is asking for ten rupees.'

'Ten rupees? Mein Gott, that is all? You tell him to come my room tonight. I will give to him one hundred rupees!'

'Tonight? Why?'

'Why? I want, that's why. Look at him. Magnificent! You tell him to come. Stay for one hour, no, two hours. This is a wonderful country . . . men like this!'

'What the hell was I supposed to do?' the guide said while all of us in office were now laughing like crazy.

'So, so,' I said, eyes streaming, 'what did you do?'

The guide took his troubles to the rest-house keeper who gave him a sympathetic hearing. He was also, very obviously, a man of the world and well versed in the idiosyncrasies of crazy tourists. 'So why didn't you tell that Andiris?' he asked.

'You're mad? How to tell things like that? I just gave him ten bucks and he buzzed off, happy as a polecat and just as gamey.'

The rest-house keeper tut-tutted. 'You should have

told him. For hundred bucks these fellows will do it up a coconut tree even.'

'Now you tell me,' said the guide bitterly. 'Can you send for this Andiris?'

'Too late now. He will get drunk with that ten rupees and then he will be useless.'

'Then what do I do? And I told the Count that I had told Andiris.'

The rest-house keeper chuckled. 'Never mind. You go and tell that German fellow that Andiris will come at eleven. Tell that he is very shy man and not to put any lights in the room. Everything must do in the dark.'

'But-but—'

'Don't worry. I'll send the cook to the room at eleven.'

By this time we were hooting our heads off. And, apparently, everything had gone off well. How true it is, I mused, that all cats are grey in the dark! Himmler rose the next day in a great state of spiritual elation. The cook hummed to himself in the kitchen. He looked, the guide remarked, as relieved as a man who had received a much-needed enema. The car was brought round. It was time to hit the road. Then Andiris sauntered in grinning something fearsome. He bowed and salaamed as Himmler slid into his seat.

'Does he want more money?' Himmler asked.

'No,' said the guide. 'I think he came to say goodbye.'

Condescendingly, Himmler nodded. Andiris nodded and asked for ten rupees. Himmler ignored the outstretched hand. They rolled out.

'My last sight was of the rest-house keeper twisting the cook's ear,' the guide said. 'Must have been trying to get a share of the hundred rupees!'

The Medical Director of the Sri Lanka Family Planning Association is a very worried woman. 'Sri Lanka is exposed to a plague that we have no control over,' she says.

But as long as countries like mine insist on parading their poverty, rich Western visitors with kinky tastes will continue to exploit the situation. All this has led to a lot of nastiness. Sri Lanka is expected to have 10,000 cases of AIDS by AD 2000. This, many say, is a very conservative estimate!

O tempora, etc., etc. etc . . . .

is exposed to a plague that we have no control over," she says.

But as long as countries like mine insist on parading their poverty, rich Western visitors with kinky tastes will continue to exploit the situation. All this has led to a lot of nastiness. Sri Lanka is expected to have 10,000 cases of AIDS by AD 2000. This, many say, is a very conservative estimate.

O tempora, etc. etc. etc.

# You Scratch My
# Back . . .

We the demigods, the bureaucrats,
We the system's tribe of scurvy rats,
We, the machine minders of the State,
Scratch our backs and we reciprocate!

In 1960 I visited the Maldive Islands. That was, considering the march of history, a long time ago. It was the kite flying season and every Maldivian male between six and sixty was engrossed in fashioning weird contraptions with coloured tissue and slivers of wood and sending them aloft where they would soar silently upon a stiff offshore breeze.

I went to the single post office where a single clerk sat behind a counter. I needed a two larees stamp. The clerk gave me a pained look. One of his hands was stuck out of the window. He signalled greeting with the other and raised a black eyebrow.

He shoved across a sheet of stamps. I detached one carefully and, with his one free hand, he pushed the rest of the sheet away, accepted my money and doled out some small coin. He didn't speak. All the while he kept shifting his gaze to the hand that was stuck out of the window. He would also arch his neck and bob his head to glance obliquely out, then resume a more human position.

I stuck on the stamp. The free hand waved me to the post box. He intrigued me the way a cat would be intrigued on seeing a mouse pushing a wheelbarrow.

Some Maldivians trooped in with sing-song voices and bad-toothed smiles. They, too, received the one-handed service. They did not seem to mind the fumblings and contortions in the fishing out of a registration tab, the daubing of some runny gum on the better part of the envelope and the awkward dispensing of small change. Very curious, I went outside, walked to the side of the building where that window was. Yes, the hand was there. It twitched occasionally. It held a spool of thread.

My post office wallah was flying a kite!

If you pause to take a studied look at the system of public administration in the Third World, you can either submit to being carried away, foaming incomprehensibly with strait-jacket and bells on, or, like millions of Third Worlders, grin and bear it. This vast bureaucratic machine is referred to as the Public Service. All who make up this vast mill, which is bunged to the ears with red tape, are called Public Servants. Note the noun. Yes, servants. They are supposed to *serve* the Public. It is for this that they are so employed, paid fat salaries, are entitled to pensions and other perks, and are a clearly favoured lot.

One of these Third World countries was hailed, in touristic posters, as a land of waving palms. The man in the street loved this description. And why not? The palms wave furiously to this day; and to get things done, one needs to grease these palms regularly. It's a noble art: you scratch my back, I'll scratch yours . . . .

It wasn't always like this, mind. Many of our countries started off with fine new brooms. A very efficient system of public administration did prevail in the pre-1950 era. The people had few grouses because they could depend on a courteous, committed public service. In fact, there were those golden days when we, the people, did not have to woo the Public Service. The public servants came to us and, with great efficiency, set things right.

Those days have been consigned to Limbo. Write to any public department today and you are considered a damn nuisance. The department also scorns reply. When you have been through the wringer you develop this insane desire to emigrate to St Pierre et Miquelon and spend the rest of your days communing with a cod fish. At least, that creature will assume an air of passing intelligence—something you don't find to any degree on the vacuous faces of public servants.

In Sri Lanka, not long ago, the Ministry of Public Administration suddenly surfaced to find that the country was losing millions because of its public servants. Poor and irregular attendance and loitering and malingering during work hours was part of the nightmare picture. In fact, the public was told to go fly a kite!

Experts dug and raised several stones to find the most unpleasant creatures skulking underneath. There were, they said, approximately 450,000 public servants in the country. These bureaucrats raked in seventy-two million rupees a day in wages (that's approximately US dollars 1.8 million) and milked the government of 56.9 million dollars every year in non-working time.

But, like the celebrated three blind mice, see how they run when there is the whiff of money. Unbelievable!

I was introduced to this phenomenon after I shipped a container of household goods from Dubai to Colombo, consigned to the tender care of American President Lines. I flew into Colombo a week earlier and went to the local shipping office.

'We will not unstuff your container in the port,' a knowing officer said. 'We will request that Customs examination be done in our own container yard.'

'What's the difference?'

'Difference? Brother, you'll be robbed blind in the port. May even pinch the container. Trust me.'

What else was there to do?

Sundry fees were paid. Use of container crane, loading of container on flatbed truck, use of said truck to carry container to private yard, use of crane to offload container at inspection site.

'Good. All done. Now we go to Customs.'

Two nattily dressed officers came up, wreathed in smiles. They examined the manifest.

'One English bath?'

'Yes.'

'I say, all these British goods heavy duty. That's not good, no? We'll say Czechoslovakian.'

'But—but how can an English bath be made in Czechoslovakia?'

'Don't worry, men, we are the Customs, no?'

Well . . . if you say so. Who's worrying?

'Now you must pay Customs deposit. How much you want to pay?'

'How about five bucks?'

'Ha, ha, you're a good joker.' Turning to his sidekick, 'He's a good joker, no?'

The other agreed. 'Ha ha ha.'

The shipping agent joined in the general merriment. 'We can go and eat lunch,' he suggested, 'and a small drink also.'

'Why not?' I agreed.

We taxied to the city for slugs of 120-proof arrack and lunch that included devilled prawns and what-the-devil-is-this beef. We Sri Lankans like our food spiced like hell-fire. The strong drink teams up with the food and stokes a volcano in the belly. Well fed, the

Customs blokes are ready to joke some more.

'You pay 15,000 rupees deposit. Come, we will go to Accounts Office.'

I am advised that this is to be a deposit against all the goods I have brought in. It is refundable, of course.

'Of course,' I agree faintly.

'Good. After that we will wait.'

The agent came up. 'You must arrange a taxi for them.'

'Why?'

'Why, to bring them to our yard. And there is an overtime payment for them also.'

'Why?'

'Because they are coming after working hours, no?'

'Working hours? But they are not working now.'

'Shhh! Their duty ends here at 4.30. After they sign off here they will come and handle your container.'

'That's normal procedure?'

'Shhh! For goodness sake don't talk like that. In the port there is no normal procedure. You tell things like that and everything will go phut!'

He left me in the Long Room. He said he would organize lorries to take my goods home after unstuffing and inspection. I mooched around. The Customs blokes staggered into the Baggage room to sleep off the arrack and devilled prawns.

By four, the agent beetled up in a beat-up taxi. At 4.30, rather rumpled and disarrayed, the Customs blokes climbed in and we bumped and ground our way to the yard. They waddled to the platform, peered into the open container and closed their eyes. This noon drinking is a painful business.

'All household goods, no?'

'Yes.'

'Good. Tell the coolies to unstuff and put in the lorries.'

The shipping agent organized this pretty deftly. By seven, with a big moon threading the clouds with orange embroidery, the lorries were ready to roll.

'Now you give us passport.'

I was nonplussed. 'My passport?'

'Yes, you give us your passport. Take the lorries and go home. Everything OK, no? You come back to the Long Room tomorrow.'

Giving up my passport I boarded the lead lorry. I waved. They waved. In convoy we roared away.

I presented myself at the Long Room the next morning. Spruce again, the Customs blokes wrung my hand warmly. 'You are a lucky man,' I was informed. 'No duty. You have foreign allowance for one year to cover your import. We made the duty to fall within your allowance. So now we can go to Accounts and you can sign a receipt for the return of your deposit.'

Dazedly, I did so. This was too good to be true. I thought of the previous evening. Where was the examination? Not a box had been opened. I could have had Ursula Andress stuffed inside that container (no pun intended). The agent had winked (or was it the moonlight?) and told me not to worry.

'Now we can go to the bar and have a small drinkie-winkie, no?'

But of course! There was cause to celebrate. These guys were the goods. My 15,000 bucks would be refunded to me and I had no duty to pay. All my goods were at home. The whole operation had been infinitely painless. The shipping agent joined us at the arrack joint. Seems it was pre-arranged.

A lot of drinkie-winkie went down the hatch. This

time it was devilled cuttle fish. I can still feel those tentacles.

Solemnly, with a hiccough that would have stopped a charging rhino, my passport was handed over.

'Now you can give us something for our trouble, no?'

The agent buzzed in my ear. 'Three thousand each will do.'

I peeled off six thousand bucks. 'Cheers.'

'Cheers.'

'More arrack?'

'Thasha . . . thass a very good idea . . . '

'Cheers!'

# *That Dread Bread Spread*

Magic mash for all our Third World bumpkins,
Even raspberries are made from pumpkins!

Jam anybody?

Lots of it around here. In bottles, jars, plastic containers, tins. Gaudy labels—strawberries like a bunch of papilloma virus, raspberries with their tongues sticking out, saying 'nyaaah!' pineapples that look as though they have had words with a cement mixer . . . .

Everywhere there is this inevitable industry. The making of jam.

That's good, says the West. Signs of progress. We newly developing nations tell the World Bank or the International Monetary Fund that lots of money is necessary. Money for jam! No big deal about feasibility studies. We have the fruit. We have the labour. We are also very excited and enthusiasm drips, dear fellow, positively drips. Funding is organized. Bottling plants, canneries, machinery for mixing and pulping, boiling and cooling vats, factories.

They're making jam with ferocious intent here. Jars with screw lids, jars with lids well jammed down, tins with that delicate cancer-blue sheen, and lo! the variety is endless. Blackberry (which is not grown here), raspberry, black currant, Victoria plum . . . . In the clear glass jar the stuff looks enticing enough. The blackberry jam has that authentic choco-purple colour; raspberry is rusty red (like last year's galvanized roofing sheets), the plum takes on a chicken-liver hue while the black currant is shockingly black. Thick, gobby jam, backed by endless television advertisements showing families wading in at breakfast with beatific smiles.

But hold hard! How the dickens does one make raspberry jam in a country that has no raspberries? In the Seventies I visited a small factory in the suburbs of Colombo to see what gives. The guy at the helm was a fat faced babu who was wrestling with a decision. 'What's a quince?' he asked.

'Temperate fruit. Does not grow here.'

'Oh. How about figs?'

'Greece and California I think. Why?'

'But there's syrup of figs in the market.'

'Yes, imported stuff. Good for babies, they say.'

'Ah,' there was a gleam in his eyes, 'then no problem. Can make some fig jam, no? What does a fig look like? Have to design a label.'

Oh brother!

Hard by was a fruit collecting centre. Like a harvest festival with bells on. Fruit flies as big as Walt Disney's Dumbo. One sees the usual: piles of squishy pineapples, mangoes with dour looks, papayas in death throes, woodapples, hog apples, silver melons and pyramids of pumpkins. Sri Lanka produces enough red pumpkin to have a Halloween bash daily.

'What's with all the pumpkins?' I asked.

'That's the base,' he said. 'Otherwise how to make jam?'

'Yes, I see, but black currant jam? From pumpkin?'

'That's the way. You'll see . . . .'

Industrialists have their trade secrets. That afternoon

I saw black currant jam in the making. REAL FRUIT JAM the label declared. A bunch of black currants and a nifty rainbow completes the design. There's even a 'best before' admonition. Ingredients carefully unlisted.

Grubby fingered girls chop and slice the pumpkins, tossing handy sized dollops into a huge vat with a mechanical stirring and squashing arm. It's pretty hot over the vat. An operator on a sort of diving board uses a face towel. In goes the water and a couple of sacks of sugar. Quite often, in goes the face towel. This is watched with interest for some time until reluctantly fished out with a metal hook on a long pole. All the while the sizzling vat is a purgatory for the fruit flies. That, one supposes, is the protein.

A sort of master chef checks for consistency. He's the fine tuner. More pumpkin, he says, or more water, or add more peel for that chunky effect. The babu yodels his satisfaction. Soon, like Old Faithful, the mess is ready to blow. It is transmogrification time. Large cans of black currant essence are tossed in. Also, as much purple dye as necessary to make the whole boiling highly carcinogenic.

'Rich in Vitamin C,' he tells me, tipping in about 2000 Celin tablets. That's just a dime a tab and does nothing to erode the profit. It's a six-hour operation. One vat fills about 1000 jars. Eureka! Black currant jam!

So OK! A bottle of this black currant jam costs the Sri Lanka housewife a dollar. But even a US dollar is a lot of rupees, and that, my friend, is pretty steep. Rich in Vitamin C, she is told; real fruit; laboratory tested and sealed under the control of some Standards Authority or another . . . and all this for a measly forty or fifty bucks. Put a jar of pure goodness on your breakfast table. Your kids will love you for it.

I'd like to use that *Sound of Music* lady. She started all this jam and bread business!

But pumpkin and fruit fly paste on bread?

Breakfast, anybody?

# *The Python Of Pura Malai*

> Full paid for by the foot, it took the floor,
> Such cabaret was never seen before,
> Away they went, not caring to applaud,
> With screams of fear and cries of Oh my God!

On Sri Lanka's north east coast, upshore of the harbour town of Trincomalee, is Nilaveli:* a peach perfect, picture postcard resort with its sugar sand beach, a creaming sea of dreamy blue and a lagoon like a sculpted topaz. Here the jungle rolls down to the Indian Ocean, hot and wet and incredibly tangled. Hook thorn vines festoon giant margosa and ironwood trees. Animarata lianas dangle in gaunt medusa heads on the tortuous branches of alstonia and ficus.

This is a wildland to lose oneself in. Ground cover is thistly and thorny, and rising in endless, boundless profusion are trees of stupendous girth and height. Wild ginger flaps sauceboat leaves in the wind which is moody and very much alive, now racing in from the sea, now voicing its oohs and ahs from the lagoon. A Tarzanesque jungle. Lianas grasp and grope in a spidery network of mottled greys and greens—an expressway for giant squirrels, grey langurs, toque monkeys and the slender loris. If tracks exist they are the tramped down paths of

---

\* The events of this story first appeared in *The Python of Pura Malai and Other Stories* (Puffin, 1995).

the wild water buffalo and the boar.

This wilderness is not for the uninitiated. The sloth bear, alone or with its mate, tearing at an anthill, will attack on sight. The leopard and its melonistic cousin, the black panther, are here, and so is that feline ball of fury, the jungle cat.

This is Nature's stage. Here, adventurers and naturalists have shot miles of film, recording the fierce wonder, the awful grandeur, the pristine glory of an untamed world: the python's coils around a young sambhur or hog deer; the frightened eyes of a chevrotain peering out of its hidey-hole in a hollow tree; the fluid beauty of spotted deer grazing in the shade of the forest's edge. This is the home of the swamp crocodile, guarding its nest between salt flat and marsh; and this is where six foot long water monitors grapple with each other, rearing on hind legs and tails to bite and gouge in their age-old rivalry battles.

It is a teeming, belling, calling jungle. The hoots of jackals, the scamper of black-naped hare, the *fluk-fluk* of a foraging pangolin, the *scrawk-skreek* of leaf monkeys argy-bargying in the trees, the *ting-ting* of palm squirrels gathering nuts in May, the whinny of the ring-tailed civet and the hissing threat of the marauding Indian palm cat.

If I would invest anyone I know in Sri Lanka with the title 'Child of Nature' it would be Reggie S. A true jungle lover with the good grace to accept the wilderness for what it is, become a part of it, add nothing to it and take nothing away from it. Reggie went to Nilaveli many years ago, liked what he saw and built himself a small house beside the sounding sea. To that haven he took his wife, raised his children, became a part of the land and melted into it. His was the happiness of a long and endearing communion with life, a forager rather than hunter, living with nature, not off it.

I joined him there, lugging necessary goods and my family and infant daughter, Minette, in a bad-tempered lorry that wheezed and snorted like a dyspeptic colonel throughout the 200-mile journey from my home in Jaela. It was a long thoughtful trek across the island. We had our work cut out for us. My family would double up with Reggie and his brood until I put up the shack that would henceforth be home. Stuff that dreams are made of, I suppose, but our sojourn in Nilaveli still remains a dazzling sunbeam in a wealth of memories.

It was no easy business, I warrant. Selecting a tract of forest glade that humped gently down to the lagoon, I made a cursory clearing for a home. Feeble, I admit, because nothing that could be cherished would be destroyed. I wasn't going to sow or reap, plough or till. I would sit under a Petromax at night and write. I would glean and beachcomb, and my children would drink buffalo milk and eat the honey from the wild beehives and there was fish aplenty. Over me, as I worked with stumping adze and axe, towered a regiment of thick-leaved Margosa and Damba (*Syzygium gardneri*). Whipsnakes flicked like light green springs from their resting places in the scleria sedge and sluggish vipers, always slow and morose in the broiling afternoon, were persuaded to take up residence elsewhere.

This was my wife's only fear. Baby girls and snakes, she said, simply do not mix. True enough. As much as I favoured this idyll of sun, sea, sand, jungle and lagoon and the fascinating diversity of life around me, I had to keep the snakes away. A nigh impossible task.

Soon, a fairly liveable structure rose to roof level. My

friends, hundreds of miles away, unanimously voted me bonkers and in dire need of psychiatric rehabilitation. While they sweated in their city offices and paraded Colombo with their briefcases and cuff-links and absurd ties, I ate ripe mulberries, caught whopping big tiger prawns with torch and handnet at nights (delicious when fried), picked lengths of agar-agar off the sea-scoured rocks for glassy jellies and lay in the lapping lagoon at dusk, soaking away the toil of the day, watching the sky grow purple and listening to the distant surf.

Reggie was all agog one evening. A seashell collector had asked him to supply five lambis—those five-pointed shells that look like breakfast rolls with fingers. 'We can pick them up at Pura Malai,' he said; and I have now to introduce you to this little outcrop in the sea—Pura Malai to the locals, which means Pigeon Island.

Pigeon Island is a devastatingly beautiful addition to the Nilaveli seascape. On one hand the sea, on the other the lagoon. Aquamarine and amethyst meet in a confluence tinged with peacock green. Beyond the Nilaveli bridge which spans the lagoon to draw the road from Trincomalee upcoast, the lagoon yawns onwards. The bridge was built in the years before World War II by the Royal Navy. And a thousand yards from the shell-strewn beach, out where the waves curdle and clamber rapturously over each other, stands Pigeon Island—a Robinson Crusoeish place with its sugarloaf central rock dome and a jade green undergrowth flowing to the water's edge.

At dawn and dusk each day, thousands of blue rock pigeons shuttle to the mainland and back. Hence the name. The pigeons live, nest and breed there, and layers of guano on the rocks witness their claim to this sea girt home. Here, too, Reggie said, are stupendously gorgeous seashells and corals: the Venus Harp, conches, helmets, murexes and cones, bespeckled cowries, file shells and argonautes.

'What's a lambis?' I asked.

'It's like an orange spider shell,' Reggie said.

I decided not to ask what an orange spider shell was.

'Lambis,' said Reggie, 'are not easy to collect. We need to dive for them. We take only five, no more, and alive. Man will only buy if the operculum is intact.'

So, we hired a vallam (a small outshore fishing boat) and pulled out to Pura Malai at dawn while the air around us whirred with the beating of pigeons heading for pickings beside the lagoon.

If I have to tell you of the enchanting treasure garden of undersea life as we secured our lambis (and I'm sorely tempted to) I will never come to our friend the python. Even as I write, I can picture it, scowling meanly, telling me to get on with my tale. 'What's a potty seashell or a whalesback of brain coral compared to the fun and games we had,' it seems to say. Well, OK, Mr Python, I'll get on, but you're rushing the muse and I proceed under protest!

We had collected our lambis, placed them at the bottom of the boat and Reggie and the boatman lay on the soft sand, both berry brown and full of contentment. I was still mucking around in the water, enjoying myself like an oversized schoolboy. Nobody noticed the python.

Suddenly, looking towards the island from five feet of water, I saw this long crepitating inner tube of a long haul truck heading towards the water. I yelled and waved frantically and Reggie, sitting up, turned, saw the python and leaped out of the way as it weaved towards him. There seemed to be no end to it. A fat, rippling river of burnt brown and ochre with the sun picking highlights of gold and chocolate on its powerful body. The boatman goggled, screamed 'Malai pambu!' (big snake) and dived into the water like Johnny Weismuller.

This, I told myself, was not the brightest of ideas. The python was making for the water too. As far as I could make out, it must have dropped in for a pigeon dinner or a pigeon egg breakfast and was now heading back to its haunts in the mainland, to the marshes beside the lagoon. And this was a great grandaddy of the Molurus species, easily fourteen feet long!

Reggie, leaping about excitedly, shouted to me, but his words were tattered in the wind. I was scrambling ashore, keeping as much distance as I could, when Reggie, seeing the python ready to take to the water, leaped out to seize it, embracing it with a fierce determination. 'Help me!' he yelled and hung on for dear life while Molurus turned, arched and opened its jaws to show rows of fierce teeth and a very threatening tongue. And it roared! One expects a snake to hiss. This was a nightmare sound: a half snarl, half bray and something like a steam cock blowing. A paralysing sound.

Visions of Reggie being pulped in the lacoon's coils spurred me to join the fray although I am still convinced I should have put the matter to higher authority before rushing in where angels fear to tread.

The boatman, too, seeing two foolhardy persons being bucked and pounded this way and that, leaped in. Soon it was a regular scrimmage with all of us riding some sort of switchback. The python, entering into the spirit of the thing, kept swishing its head and trying to close its jaws on anything human that hove into view.

Suddenly, we were all in the water and while a large segment was tying a loveknot around my waist, Reggie had performed a desperate hand over hand and was now gripping the creature's neck and actually trying to straddle it. Up and down he went, like a coconut plucker in a cyclone, slapping water furiously. The boatman was obviously contending with the mid-section. He kept coming up for air, blowing like a whale and then disappearing in a mass of froth. His shirt was in tatters and great red weals stood up on his brown back.

'He's weakening,' Reggie cried in a blubbery way. 'Hang on and strike for the beach.'

Neatly put. But what beach? We were now about a hundred yards away from Pigeon Island. My body stung all over. I felt the bite of sea water in places where the skin was raw and scored. My ribs hurt, my shoulders hurt and that tail kept giving me six of the best at every opportunity.

I didn't know what had possessed Reggie to trifle with this monster. His right arm was bleeding. He had received an angry bite. Slowly, we steered the python towards the mainland where a bunch of scallywags who had come to dynamite for fish also leaped in to help. The boatman staggered ashore, smote his head, howled to the palms that his boat was at Pura Malai and lay on the sand kicking out despairingly. Someone brought a large jute sack and the python was jacked in, where it must have asked, like the man who had been hit by a runaway bullet train, 'What happened!'

Reggie grinned and said, 'Ouch!'

I didn't grin back. We now had this bejesus of a python in a sack and what, I burned to know, was the big, painful idea? My back ached. My spine, I told him, felt as though it had been worked on by a troop of Boy Scouts practising knots. My ribs felt like putty and there were angry red stripes on the side of my neck and across my shoulders. Reggie was in worse condition and he said his arm throbbed like the blazes.

'Good,' I said unfeelingly, 'now open that sack and let that thing go.'

He was shocked. 'Let it go? After all this? I promised the hotel a python.'

It had so happened that the manager of a beach hotel had asked Reggie to supply him with a python which could be caged for display to tourists. Reggie had made mention one day that he had lost a lot of his pullets to a visiting python and the manager had suggested that Reggie catch that python and bring it to him.

Reggie had said OK, and the manager had said good. Reggie had asked how much and the manager had said, airily, five hundred, and Reggie had looked very huffed and invited the manager to get into the cage himself. An interesting conversation had followed with some Little and Large crosstalk. Reggie had pointed out that a big hotel needs a big python even if it had only a pint-sized manager and the manager had said who's pint-sized, and Reggie had said there, there, soothingly. He then suggested that the manager pay by the linear foot.

They had considered this over two bottles of beer and the manager had said OK, fifty bucks per foot and Reggie had said the bigger the python the harder to catch and why doesn't the manager get a pair of mongoose instead.

All this led to more beer and the manager had mellowed to a point where the ante had been raised to one hundred and fifty rupees per foot, 'But I want a big python, do you hear?' and Reggie had said bingo and promised early delivery.

'So that's how it is,' I said. 'But I don't like it one bit. Caging a beauty like this just to show tourists.'

Reggie closed one eye slowly. 'That manager

fellow . . . pompous little bugger. You think I'm going to hand him our friend on a plate? I've sent some of those fellows to shout the glad news. Ghent to Aix style. By now everyone within five miles will know we have this huge python. I'd say he's about fourteen feet. Let's see . . . 150 bucks a foot . . . that's 2100 rupees. Just play along, right?'

The boatman rose. 'I go bring boat,' he said dolefully.

'And my shells,' Reggie reminded.

The man dipped back into the water, giving the bulging sack a vile look.

'I've got to put something on this bite,' Reggie murmured.

The beach hotel was not far away. Just walk along the strand and there rise the pillars around a sort of sun deck with tables and beer-swilling Norwegians and a miniature bar. Beyond rises the hotel proper but nobody comes from Europe to an Asian beach resort to stay in a room. The tourists in their exclamation mark bikinis and large brimmed straw hats, hang around the water, the patio, the outer lounge. Outside this sundeck were cages where the manager already held a toque monkey and a porcupine in thrall.

Yes, the glad tidings had reached him. He stood, rubbing his hands as we approached, limping, dragging the sack along the soft sand. Behind us came a regular procession of local yokels who were jabbering like macaws at a peanut convention.

'Two thousand bucks,' said Reggie, 'and bring out your first aid box. This is a fourteen footer.'

'Yes, yes, people told me. My, our visitors will love this. Can you put it in the cage?'

'Antiseptic first. Boy, I'm bushed. Look at that bite.

See the marks on my back. If we hadn't dragged it into the sea it would have got away.'

'But you can't leave it there.'

'Why not? It can't go anywhere. You want me to die of some bloody infection?'

We went to his office where Reggie dabbed his wounds with Dettol and made sure to collect two crisp one thousand rupee notes.

'You're sure it's fourteen feet?'

'Sure I'm sure. You go and measure it.'

The manager hastily declined. 'Just put it in the cage.'

The sundeck was now brimming over with tourists of every make and model. Some were breakfasting. Some were drowsing over glasses of orange juice. Others were lathering each other's backs with oils and lotions while yet others were simply mincing around in bathing suits that never got wet.

Reggie winked. 'Stand back,' he hissed. 'There's going to be hell on wheels in the next couple of seconds.' He made as though to lift the sack upright and slipped the knot in the rope. One hears of the spring of jack rabbits. Our python had every jack rabbit pipped at the post. It shot out of the sack and, needless to say, it was in a very bad mood. I yelled. Reggie yelled . . . but these cries of encouragement were but puny whimpers to the roars of anguish, howls of terror, that rose to gale force around us. The tourists and hotel staff in a body were intent on putting as much territory as possible between themselves and this fearsome thing that had suddenly appeared like the Assyrian from the fold.

The smooth polished floor made matters worse. The python couldn't muster the traction desired to get it away into the wide open spaces. It slipped, it skidded, it weaved, it plunged here, there, everywhere, while the diaspora climaxed and legs pumped energetically and some bolted until they were half way to Trincomalee and others shinned up tables and bawled for mother.

The python, not to be outdone, toppled chairs and writhed under tables, sliding crossly around until it decided to hump itself and thus gain leeway. All the while the manager did a puppet act behind the bar and shouted, 'Catch it! Catch it!' while a shapely Danish girl, half way up a trellis, kept screaming, 'Kill it! Kill it!'

Reggie seized a pole.

'Put it in the cage!' the manager roared, doing a sort of polka.

'I can't,' Reggie roared back. 'My arm's stiff,' and with the help of the pole he eased the thoroughly bewildered reptile off the floor into the garden where it doubtless gave an 'aah' of relief and shot off to the sanity of its own world.

The rest was silence. For a few seconds anyway. The shapely tourist slid down the trellis, took a deep breath and decided that it was time to faint. She did, and the manager rallied round with a soda siphon. Recovery was near miraculous.

'Where's my money?' the manager demanded.

'You mean you want your money back?' Reggie gave him a pained look.

'You let the python go!'

'Maybe. But you paid me to bring a python. So I brought. That's that, end of contract. All executed to mutual satisfaction, no? Now how much are you going to pay me for letting it go?'

Despite my aching ribs I was laughing my head off.

This put the flustered manager into a steam kettle mood. 'Who's he? What's he laughing at?'

'Just look at us,' Reggie grinned. 'What a damn silly bunch we are! You. Look at you. Your job is to run a hotel. And you're buying pythons. And where are your guests? Still running? And look at this place. Like a café in Belfast. I'll tell you what? Let's eat. Nothing like a good breakfast, no? Ham and eggs, toast, marmalade, grapefruit, coffee—not espresso. That's the least you can do for all the trouble we have had.'

'Trouble?' the manager hooted. 'What about this place? What about my customers? I'll have to scour the country for them. And will they stay after this, with a bloody big python around here somewhere? Where did it go?'

'Maybe the honeymoon suite. No telling with pythons.'

'And you want breakfast? You wreck my hotel, chase away my guests—'

'So I'll pay. I have money.'

'That's my money!'

'Oh very well, I'll give you back your money.'

'Wassat?'

'You heard me. Who wants your money anyway . . . but a good breakfast, ah, that's something else.'

So we ate. Slap-up breakfast too; and we sat on the sun deck and gazed towards Pura Malai that lay like a burnished opal in the sun. Peace tucked its quilt around us. Somewhere a puzzled python was doubtless telling the missus that it was a mad, mad world and he was going to lay off pigeons for a while.

Reggie collected his lambis and we walked home. The manager watched us go ruefully. 'Maybe I should put some rabbits in the cage,' he said.

'Or guinea fowl,' Reggie suggested. 'They hate snakes.' He rubbed his tummy, looked around, saw no witnesses and gave a loud, satisfied belch . . . .

*Confucius He*
*Say . . .*

Chin chin Chinaman, velly led in face,
Flag of other Chinaman velly big disglace!

China and Taiwan don't like each other. Funny business, this. They're all Chinese.

Frederick Pittera, a tough New Yorker, was President of the World Trade and Expo Centre in Sharjah, United Arab Emirates in the 1980s. He bit down on his cigar and scowled at me. 'You're sure there won't be a mess-up,' he asked for the sixty-seventh time.

I was his Vice President, International Sales, in the toughest selling job in the world. I had quit the *Gulf News,* Dubai to team up with Fred as his Press Officer. What the heck? He summoned me one day, gave me a rare grin and said: 'Whatever the newspaper is paying you, I'll double it!' But somewhere along the line I took over Sales and immediately became cook, valet and bottlewasher. The answer was stress tabs.

Selling trade exhibition space is nothing to wave flags and cheer about. You sell empty space—15,000 square metres of it—at US$ 150 per square metre. Try that in your saner moments. And Fred had a heavy trade fair calendar. Ten major fairs in six months. That was the average.

Now, a big international Expo was almost upon us and the floor plan had these two pavilions, enthusiastically labelled CHINA and TAIWAN.

'Side by side,' Fred groaned. 'And I thought you were

a newspaper man. Don't you know anything about Far Eastern politics?'

'They're coming here to trade,' I reminded stubbornly, 'not to hold a summit.'

'Huh! That's all you know. We are going to have a bloody international incident! I can feel it! Moon must be in Scorpio.'

The Chinese International Trade Caucus had a 900 square metre pavilion. An advance team was already in Sharjah to design their exhibition area. Colourful archways, red banners, chrome and glass display units, lots of hammering and drilling and bobbing around in blue pants and jackets. Busy little beavers, charming, courteous.

In charge was Go Jing Gong of the Beijing Exhibition Board. I called him Jigalong and he beamed. He claimed to be a big brass in Fu Xing Men Wai Street where his department was housed. I introduced him to Paul R. Martin, a visiting American. Paul was Student Director on the Thunderbird Campus, Glendale, Arizona, and he considered the Chinese team thoughtfully. 'If only we could get our people to work like this,' he said. 'Just look at 'em. And they're officials. Not labourers. It's a lesson for us all.'

The exhibitors came in. It was ulcer time. Austrians, Germans, Hungarians, heaping portions of Indians and Pakistanis, Greeks, Lebanese, Spaniards, Turks, a sprinkling of Britishers, Somalis gabbling in French, some Dutch, a hysterical Kenyan who was sure his two wives would bolt in his absence, Filipinos, Malaysians, South Koreans, a Bhutanese who wrung everybody's hand and said, 'I am ver' poor man. You give me discount pliss.'

Nobody bothered about the Taiwan pavilion. Leader George Han was a wealthy industrialist at the helm of

Taipei's Ferocious Corporation.

'What gives George?' I had telexed, and back came a voluble reply: 'Don't worry. We arrive. Soon. Bringing heavy machinery. Thirty companies. Remember have sign REPUBLIC OF CHINA not TAIWAN and our national flag outside pavilion.'

Reasonable enough. The fair ground had flagpoles for the hoisting of all national flags.

'You,' barked Fred, 'are like a cow pissing on a flat rock. You can't handle everything. Delegate some of this stuff and concentrate on the Chinese and George Han. You sold. You're responsible!'

I summoned the Chinese. 'We will have a Taiwanese pavilion as well,' I said.

'What? Here?'

'Where else?'

Lots of yips and yaps in Chinese. Sing-song notes of protest. Umbrage in contralto.

'Gentlemen, please. You have come here to trade. Shall we shove the politics?'

Jing Gong gave a sharp bow. 'We will discuss this and return.'

They held a pow-wow outside their pavilion.

Just then the Bien Venue bus rolled in and out popped George Han and a horde of Taiwanese. George was a burly fellow. 'How are you, how are you,' he roared. 'Where is our flag? What are those Chinese doing on the grounds? Are you hiring cheap labour?'

'And who is this Chinese bellowing in my office?' I countered. 'You're Chinese, aren't you?'

'I'm R.O.C. Republic of China,' he insisted and carolled to the rest of the group who immediately invaded the sanctum. Passports were tossed on my desk. Bags dumped on every inch of floor space. 'Come,' George roared, 'we look at our pavilion. You come and show us?'

After the tour we all returned tight-lipped. Several Taiwanese corks were about to pop. George opened his mouth. I held up a warning hand. 'Now just you listen. You have come here as a private trade group. You've come, you've paid, and your exhibition material is being unloaded in the port. All this effort . . . and now you want to fuck it all up with politics? Ignore those Chinese. Sell your stuff, invite the whole of the UAE to Taipei if you wish. Do your thing and go home.'

'And what about our flags'

'They will be hoisted.'

'And you will call our pavilion the REPUBLIC OF CHINA hall?'

'Assuredly.'

'And those bloody Chinese?'

'What about them?'

'Will they give us trouble?'

'Why should they?'

'You don't know these bloody Chinese,' he said darkly.

'Oh, I think so. I'm looking at one.'

'What do you mean? I'm Republic of China!'

'Sez you. Here's your passport. See . . . George Han. Nationality Chinese.'

'But there is big difference!'

I sighed. 'I suppose so. A big stupid difference.'

'You are insulting!' he roared.

'Exactly. And don't shout. You're making my secretary nervous. The last time she got nervous do you know what she did? She threw a box file at a fat Jordanian. Now listen, George, you're my friend, right? But if you don't like this fair just bug off. It's up to you. I'll give your pavilion to the Chinese. They'll welcome the extra space.'

I led him to the coffee machine. 'Have a cup. Then you can pack up and go away and sue me.'

Hardly had George stalked off when Jing Gong jigged in. He gave a small bow and arranged his team around my table. 'We will permit Taiwanese to stay,' he said, 'but you will not call their pavilion REPUBLIC OF CHINA . You can say TAIWAN .'

'I see. And what else do you or do you not permit?'

'Ah yes. No Taiwanese flags on the grounds.'

At this stage I thought about that cow and the flat rock. Concentrating on these Chinese was doing me no good. It encouraged ulcers. I smiled carefully. It had to be that sort of disarming smile before I led him to a great height, showed him a flat rock far below and said that he should consider himself a trickle of cow piss. 'Very well. Now I will permit all of you to pack up and leave. Please stop all work and go to your hotel. I will ask CAAC to provide seats on the first available flight. Your passports will be handed to you at the airport. Now, if you will excuse me, I must see about cancelling your visas.'

Who said offence is the best defence? I love that guy. The Chinese opened their mouths and forgot to close them for some time. I strode out and sneaked into Fred's office.

'What's going on?' he asked.

'Not much. I told all the Chinese to go home.'

'God Almighty! Now they'll start fighting in the streets!'

'Don't worry. They'll all buckle down and be good little boys. Like to bet?'

'Bet? That's a Chinese government trade team. You gone bats or something?'

Jing Gong poked a head in. His grin froze when he saw me, but he was determined to appeal to higher authority. Half an hour later he had learned that there was no Chinese diplomatic representation in the UAE while there was a Taiwanese ambassador knocking around. Slowly, and with no remorse whatsoever, I chipped away at the pile of bricks he was standing on. High dudgeon was sent to the cooler. 'At least don't put REPUBLIC OF CHINA sign,' he pleaded.

Fred wreathed him in a cloud of cigar smoke. 'So what's the problem? You are Peoples Republic of China. That's good. Republic with people. These other guys are Republic of China. Without people. What sort of a Republic is that, for Chrissake!'

Jing Gong thawed. Remarks like this were music to his ears. 'But it is still problem,' he maintained.

'I think there is a way out,' I said. 'You've already got your sign up. Right. I've checked the stores and we are running out of plastic lettering. There are not enough letters to repeat REPUBLIC OF CHINA again and again for the Taiwanese pavilion.'

'Now I'll have Han in here,' Fred moaned.

Jing Gong cracked his jaws open. The wide smile showed me that he favoured gold teeth. 'If you cannot put sign then why you are going to cancel our visas?'

'Oh, I have letters. We are short of I's, A's and E's. So I have ordered ROC  PAVILION.'

Fred hmmmmd. Jing Gong dropped the shutters over his teeth. He was considering whether it would be better to go home and make rude noises at Hong Kong.

'Now listen,' I said, 'you'll thank me for this. Really. This is an Arab country, right?'

He nodded.

'Good. And all Arabs know what a roc is.'

'Excuse me, I do not follow. What is this roc?'

'Aha! There are you! What about the old Arab story of Sindbad the Sailor? There was this monster bird. Called

70

a roc. Big, ugly bird. What'll happen when all the Arab buyers see this ROC PAVILION? They will not like it. So your hall may have more business, right?'

There was an instant sunrise of gold teeth. 'Why did you not tell this to me before? I must go and tell my people about this roc. Big bird? And ugly? That is very good. When I go back and make my report I will tell this story.'

We parted buddy-buddies.

George Han was in two minds. 'Can't you order some letters?' he whined. 'ROC PAVILION sounds like an all-night disco.'

'Sorry, George, we are out of letters. Tell you what? I'll make it PAVILION OF ROC.'

That, George declared, was better. 'Just space out between R and O and C,' he said.

I thought the last hurdle had been cleared. The Fair opened and everything went smoothly until George rushed in. 'Our flags are gone! This is sabotage!'

Back to the coffee machine.

I found out that the Chinese had paid a little Indian to snaffle the flags. While opening ceremonies held everyone's attention, the lackey had hauled down the Taiwanese flags and spirited them away. Gatekeeper Ahmed had a story to tell. The Chinese had arrived outside the gates and Jing Gong had cased the joint with a pair of field-glasses. Ahmed had invited them in. Jing Gong had stayed put. 'If the Taiwan flag is flying we will not go in,' he had declared while the others said Amen in Chinese. The Indian was pushed in, however, bearing assorted boxes. Later, said Ahmed, the Indian had come back with a bulky parcel. Jing Gong made a swift recheck, smiled satisfaction and led his troops in.

Han was furious. He wanted the flags replaced.

'Tomorrow,' I soothed, 'and I will post guards at the flagpoles.'

An hour later the Chinese swept in. 'We are insult!' Jing Gong cried. 'Damn Taiwanese wave flags at us!'

'What do you mean wave flags at you? They have no flags to wave. You pinched their flags!'

'Never! Why for we want the traitor flag?'

'To burn in your hotel room I suppose.'

He scorned reply. 'What do you do about all these flags?'

'What flags?'

'Taiwan flags! Millions of flags! They wave at us!'

'Must be quite a breeze. Where?'

'In Taiwan pavilion.'

'So it's their pavilion.'

'But they wave at us! Inside and now outside also!'

This I had to see. Inside the Taiwan pavilion, in every exhibition stand, on every desk and counter, hundreds of little desk-top Taiwan flags. George grinned.

'So you came prepared,' I said.

'Yes,' he said happily. 'Bloody Chinese in a panic.'

'You can't go around sticking these flags under every Chinese nose,' I objected.

'Who says so? We have right to dress up our stands. Now everybody knows this is Republic of China.'

He was right. Every exhibit, the machinery, the lathes and grinders, knitting machines, bottle cappers, whatever, were festooned with small flags. Visitors and trade buyers were given Taiwan flags to take away. The Chinese, with no such ammo were fast assuming the appearance of flounders on a salt flat.

But not for long. Even as I spoke with George, a large wedge of Chinese barged in, each with a long-stemmed yellow artificial flower. They treaded their way, pausing at every stand. This was fell purpose with a capital P. They gestured rudely at the Taiwanese with their yellow flowers.

George Han's eyes bulged. 'This is bloody insult!' he roared, seized a hand flag and waved it furiously. Soon, all the Taiwanese were waving their flags frantically while the Chinese hopped and skipped around brandishing their yellow flowers. My God, I thought, they're putting a hex on each other. But it was a sight for sore eyes and vastly entertaining at that.

Frederick Pittera sent for me around closing time. 'Saw something peculiar. Very peculiar. Flags and flowers all over the place. You know what's going on?'

'Me? I'm desk bound. Loads of stuff to get through.'

He champed on his cigar. 'How are the Chinese?'

'Slit eyed. Slightly slant.'

He sighed. 'And the Taiwanese?'

'Ditto.'

'What the hell are you not telling me?'

'Trust me,' I begged. 'I'll have all loose ends tucked away tonight.'

That night I took a team of ground staff and searched both pavilions. Every hand flag, every yellow flower was confiscated and brought to the office. Fred had knocked up some storage out of old shipping containers. The stuff was tossed in and the doors locked.

First visitor the next day—George Han. 'All our flags have been stolen!'

'Good. Relax. Have some coffee. You can sell everything but your country's flag.'

'But—'

'But what? There's the coffee.'

No word from the Peoples Republic of China. The Fair progressed. Both sides appeared to have called a truce.

Late nights don't make for endearments from the wife. I had been getting inscrutable looks, dirty Chinese looks.

Confucius he say: He who wave flag and flower have no time to throw bomb!

# Go, Man, Go!

Drilled to death! This Navy round forsooth!
Soap can ease your day in ways uncouth!

Join the navy and see the world, they said!

Join the navy and have a girl in every port, they said!

Pshaw! I was given an outlandish .303 rifle with a warped stock and told to march, all the while carrying said rifle on my left shoulder. Months and months of this!

'What the hell is the use of this uniform if we don't go to sea?' growled Ordinary Signalman Simmons one day.

Which we endorsed as a very telling observation.

Grabbing a bus home we would meet some most disquieting situations:

'Hello, sailor,' someone would say, 'been to England? Settle this argument for us, will you? Is Bedford in the north or south?' Or: 'Been abroad?' Or: 'Ever been in Singapore?'

One of our mob was a regular romancer. He also knew his geography and was most convincing about the places he hadn't gone to. 'England's a grand old place,' he would nonchalantly tell a fellow traveller. 'I'm lucky to have been around so much. Really sailed the seas. You name it, I've sailed it. Why, this is the first time I've been ashore for any real length of time.'

'Oh really?' his companion would say. 'I wish I had your luck.'

'Well, it's no picnic, I can tell you. Lots of hard work,

being a sailor. But say, haven't I seen you somewhere before?'

'Could be, but tell me, ever been to the Trucial Coast?'

'Trucial Coast? Every inch of it. Basrah, Bahrain, Oman, Yemen. All very rich. Oil, you know.'

'How about East Africa?'

'Kilindi, Nairobi, Zanzibar—right down to Joburg. That's what we say for Johannesburg. I'm sure I have seen you somewhere before.'

'Oh, I must get off here. Mind ringing the bell? Thanks,' and leaning a little closer the man would say, 'See me in the Petty Officers Mess tomorrow, sailor boy. Yes, come straight in and ask for Chief Petty Officer Jansen. That's me!'

'I went home in a daze,' he told us later while we laughed till we developed stitches.

'So what happened, you bloody lunatic?'

Quite a lot had happened in the PO's mess the next day. The poor chap had been brought before a gathering of petty officers and chief petty officers, introduced as Sindbad the Sailor and made to relate the story of his many voyages. After a gruelling morning he had been well thumped and booted out to the accompaniment of loud catcalls and howls of derision.

But really, something had to be done about all this marching, marching, left turns and about turns and having to listen to a litany of insults from the cretin who pranced behind us with a very red face and a mad light in his eyes. It was decided that the situation could be eased somewhat by reporting sick. But first, a way of falling ill had to be discovered. It was Electricians Mate Aloysius who hit on the idea of swallowing soap and washing it down with mugfuls of warm water. It worked, for Aloysius was soon a going concern. He was removed to the Army Hospital by shocked Sick Bay Attendants.

This was too good to be true. Soap was swallowed at random. Signalman 'Daft' Fernando even drank a mug of shaving water. By eight a.m. we were all crowding the Medical Reception Station of the Army Hospital.

'Purging,' said an Army medical orderly to the staff sergeant, 'the whole bloody Navy is purging.'

'So why are they here?' scowled the Staff. 'There are no lavatories in their camp?'

The Captain, Ceylon Army Medical Corps, did not seem to like us either. 'You!' he barked at Ordinary Seaman Deen. 'What did you eat this morning?'

Deen began to count off on his fingers. 'A loaf of bread, two sausages, four eggs, four cups of tea, half a bottle of tomato sauce, three boiled potatoes, a packet of cream crackers, a glass of orange juice and a mango.'

'Jeeesus! Is that a stomach or a bloody tub? Who the fuck issues victuals in your mess?'

Deen grinned. 'I get two extra eggs, sir, because I am a Muslim and I don't eat sausages.'

'But you just said you ate two sausages!'

'Yes, sir, they were beef sausages, so I ate.'

The Captain closed his eyes. 'No wonder you buggers are purging,' he breathed. 'I'll be in the loo for a week if I ate like that.' He turned on the Staff with a grimace. 'I want to examine their stools,' he said. 'Four bloody eggs.' He looked at Deen with near wonder. 'Packet of cream crackers, loaf of bread . . . Jeeesus! Give them each a mug of black coffee. No sugar, no milk, like bloody tar!' He stomped out but turned at the door. 'There are only six lavatories here. I don't want a bloody stampede. If you bastards soil this place I'll run you all out with a fucking bayonet!'

We were given a dinky little ceramic bedpan each and ordered to present samples of naval waste when the urge was next upon us. This we did docilely enough. Being in the MRS was a relief anyway. We thought of the others marching around the parade ground and smirked. There were disadvantages, however. No food. The Staff was emphatic. 'If you buggers eat lunch on top of all that breakfast we'll have to build new lavatories!'

Nobody questioned his judgement. The soap had done its worst and the rumbles in our bellies had dropped to hoarse whispers. Like a floor polisher being used in the far corner of a room.

It was two in the afternoon when the bomb went off. A very volatile Captain stormed into the ward. He foamed, yes, foamed—as though he had swallowed a bar of soap himself.

'Malingerers!' he howled and stamped his feet. Both feet . . . and very quickly. Like the mating dance of a prairie chicken. A spell binding performance, more so because he held a bed pan in his left hand. What he next said was in such croaking fury that nobody could understand a word. Then, dropping the vaudeville he advanced on us with a wild light in his eyes. He checked the tag on the bedpan. 'Who is A-550?' he hissed. I sat up in bed and gave him my best long-suffering look. Mona Lisa would have been a close runner-up.

'Get out of that bed this minute! Get out! Get out!'

I got out. If he had told me to fly to the moon I would have done so and never paused to ask why. Comply and complain. That's what the armed forces teaches you.

'What did you eat this morning?'

'Bread and eggs, sir.'

A long intake of breath. 'I see. Only bread and eggs?'

'Yes, sir.'

'Not soap?'

'Sir?'

'Soap! Soap! S-O-P-E-soap!'

'Oh, soap?'

'What do you mean oh soap? Either it's yes soap or no soap. Not oh soap!' He fought for wind and then burst out again: 'Did you eat soap?'

'Soap, sir?'

'Will you answer my question you runt of misery!' (Only he didn't say 'runt'.)

'Yes, sir.'

'Well?'

'I didn't eat soap, sir.'

'So you didn't, eh? Come here! Look at this!' pointing a quivering finger at the bed pan. 'What is this?'

'Shit, sir.'

'I know that! And it's yours! Do you know what's in it? Soap! So you didn't eat soap—but you shit soap! You're a cute little bunch of bastards, aren't you? Eat soap, start purging and come here to lie on my beds. Out! All of you, out!'

We were all out of bed anyway. The big scheme had come unstuck. Worse still, we were still loose around the sphincters. The Captain was telephoning the Navy Commanding Officer. 'Send a truck for this lot. There's nothing wrong with them . . . yes, yes, they need extra drill, extra work, extra punishment and an extra kick in the backside . . . no, I can't kick them for you. Some of them are still purging . . . OK . . . no sweat at all . . . only watch out for this lot, they're hell on wheels . . . '

He turned on us with a face that twisted repugnantly.

'Get dressed and don't ever come here again! Not even if you're dying! So help me God, I'll give anyone who comes here again a thousand cc's of formalin! You know what happens when you get a thousand cc's of formalin?'

We could have guessed. There was no need to rub it in.

'He gets stiff. He's a well-preserved corpse! A bloody waxwork! And you know where the formalin is injected? Up your bloody arses!' He swept out in a clatter of boots and harness.

Brrr! The sadists who masquerade as Army doctors!

# God  Equals  Claud

> We journalists are oft a crazy crowd.
> We do our worst, and do it clear and loud;
> But happenstance makes all this fall apart,
> Without a paper, where's that old black art?
> We went to work . . . is this some kind of fraud?
> There was no paper—only Malcolm Claud!

Not long ago, Dubai was a small enclave of semi-literate traders, the ancestors of the dissidents from the Bani Yas tribe who had quit Abu Dhabi to set up their own community.

Inter-family slaughter, assassinations, eye-gougings and other forms of mayhem were quite a pastime. Those who survived such tender attentions were usually banished a few miles down the desert to Sharjah.

In his book, *Farewell to Arabia* (Faber and Faber, 1966), David Holden quotes how warring factions used to open up on each other with 300-year-old cannons plugged with rags and loaded with pistons stolen from hijacked cars. He said that cannonballs generally were in such short supply that a truce was declared after sunset prayers to enable both sides to comb the battlefield for old balls that might be used again the next day.

My first morning in Dubai began at the unearthly hour of five, since, having arrived at four-thirty, there was no point in going to sleep. At nine, we had been informed, cars would come to swoop us away to the offices of the *Gulf News*. This raised a characteristic Sri Lankan protest. 'What? Nine o'clock? But we arrived at four-thirty. They should give us the morning off!'

The owner of the *Gulf News* hadn't thought of that. A wealthy and important Arab, he had launched into the newspaper business with the firm intention of giving an already established daily, the *Khaleej Times*, a run for its money. He was young, and an idealist. He already ran a nice little printing business and it was thus a natural progression to put out a newspaper.

His name was Abu and he also believed in running a business in the slow, orthodox manner of the older generation of trading Arabs. It was a shock to us to be told on arrival at the office that the *Gulf News* was not in circulation. It had been temporarily stopped, explained editor Jim Headgear, but he did not elaborate.

'So we have no work to do?' I remarked.

Headgear looked at his watch rather self-consciously. 'It's been a setback,' he said. 'We had to dismiss a large number of the staff. You are the replacements. Now I'll introduce you the Chief Sub-editor, Malcolm Claud, and he will get you chaps organized.'

What had happened to the *Gulf News* had been simply that Abu had set up his newspaper along lines which were quite characteristic of any business undertaking in those days. He went to England for the staff and expertise he needed. Recruiting an editor and a team of British journalists at tremendous cost, he laid out a small fortune in meeting all their terms and conditions and then sat back to watch his paper apply a half-Nelson on the market.

It was the general pattern. Many Arabs, even today, feel that a European should be General Manager or hold top post. Thus, they feel that they have given their business a 'touch of class'. Abu did just this. In the lower echelons were the Asians. The editorial department was the preserve of the whites.

Today, most Arabs have overcome this complex. They have come to recognize the 'cowboy' and have increasingly turned to Asia and the Far East for manpower. It used to be different fifteen years ago. A stratified society was being built up in the Gulf States.

At the top were the pukka sahibs who even had their own pubs in Dubai and Sharjah and did a 'Rupert Brooke' wherever they went. They clung grimly to the concept that they had been lords and masters of the Gulf not so long ago and should be treated thus *ad nauseam*. It would not be wrong to sum up the pattern of these European operations thus: 'Get that mountain moving. We shall take it to Mohammed!'

Safaris to the Middle East were deployed along old familiar lines: a quick weekend in Teheran to soak the then Shah for a few millions; drop in on the king of Saudi Arabia and give him some expensive advice; and those Bedouin in the UAE distribute money and watches to everyone—should be an interesting day or two . . . these Arabs have money and it's a bit of a shame, what, if we don't take as much of it away from them as possible!

Not long ago one of America's banks suggested in the grand manner that it should 'handle' the whole of Saudi Arabia's oil revenue, and sent experts from New York to plan the kingdom's future. American University presidents would travel to Iran in increasing numbers seeking endowments. They were so successful that Japanese electronics companies began to disguise their salesmen as professors, sending them to the Middle East to talk scholastics, but really to sell audio-visual equipment!

I have no doubt that all over the developed world—in New York, London, Frankfurt, Tokyo, Paris, Zurich, the printing industry boomed as millions of glossy brochures were churned out for carriage to the Middle East. The appeal was to the *noveau riche* Arab. Whatever the gew-gaw, the system, the do-it-yourself culture kit, it was the quickest way 'to bring the UAE (or Qatar or Kuwait) into the 21st century' or they were products or technology that would provide 'awareness or technology or education all up and down the social scale'. Scruples had nothing to do with it.

In its own small way, the *Gulf News* came to a grinding halt with the rodeo tactics of the British cowboys. In Malcolm Claud's filing cabinet was a stack of glossy photographs which had been specially flown in from London for the newspaper. They were 'Page Three Girls'. Abu had really spun his wheels when he saw a page proof with Betty Bloxham of Surrey wearing nothing but a smile. Sadly, Claud realized that he was no longer in some hole in the wall in Fleet Street.

Sadder still, the cowboys realized that this could never be an English newspaper as they had hoped to make it. So they let it go to pot. Abu saw his dreams tatter. He upped and sacked the lot and told Jim Headgear to go East. 'Bring me journalists from Asia,' he said. Headgear came to Sri Lanka.

Having taken all this in and introduced ourselves to the coffee machine, we resolved our duties and waited interestedly for Claud to open his mouth. He did, and it cooked his goose as far as we were concerned.

'I am Claud,' he said, 'Malcolm Claud. I am the Chief

Sub-editor. I'd like you to get one thing clear. I am never wrong. And even if you think I am wrong, I am more right than anybody else!'

Lateef Farouk tipped me a wink.

'We had someone in Colombo who said much the same thing,' I said.

'Oh really? Was he a chief sub?'

'No. He was in the bloody lunatic asylum.'

Claud let that go. Nihal Kaneira leaned forward, ready to do battle. It was an unpromising start.

'I can see that none of you have any idea about computer setting or any experience of how a modern newspaper is produced,' Claud said. 'It has put me into a bit of a hole, because Jim promised me he would bring experienced staff. Now I will have to tell Abu that we cannot re-start.'

'You mean we are not going to produce a paper?' Dudley Fernando asked.

'Not yet. You will have to be trained first.'

G.W. Surendra told me in Sinhala: 'This is a load of bull. In Colombo we produced papers like mosquitoes.'

'But,' I reminded, 'he's never wrong.'

Surendra snorted. 'Then he can't be Claud. Must be God!'

It was Lateef who took up the cudgels. He just sailed into Abu's office and laid it on the line. Abu listened and nodded gravely. 'I have announced that on the 23rd of March the *Gulf News* will be on the streets. It will be so,' he said simply.

We had a pow-wow. Can we do it? 'We can,' I said, 'but Claud is not ready to risk it.'

As we saw it, if the paper did not come out on 23 March, Abu may decide to scrap it altogether. We may all have had to go back. The thought was a disquieting one.

But we did not reckon on the character of the Bedouin. The character of Abu . . .

In ancient days, the countries of the Arabian Gulf did not lack a civilization. In fact, its indigenous civilization may have lasted longer in its original form than probably any other developed civilization. The first Arabs were the nomads who roamed the deserts of the peninsula, evolving a crude form of clan society where survival was the name of the game.

With the acknowledgement that safety lay in numbers, the clan concept was furthered, developed into a strong entity. A notable feature of clan kinship was the 'blood tie' which bound all members together in a sort of spiritual bond.

Later, anthropologists say, the clan concept developed into a tribal system which pursued two basic forms of livelihood: grazing flocks and herds and raiding settlements, especially along the coasts. It was by dint of this latter practice of raiding that they were called Bedou: Nomads who had the additional distinction of being raiders, which, after all, was a most profitable pastime.

Many of the customs, practices and instincts of early Bedouin life passed down the centuries to become an intrinsic part of the modern Arab character. I was soon to realize this. The desert has bred a fierce independence and a governing sense of superiority. Even at the beginning of the Christian era, Bedou society was secure in the traditional knowledge that it constituted the natural aristocracy of the Middle East—superior by far to all who had come and gone in the desert's turbulent history, and superior to the foreigners who came in increasing numbers to their lands.

Malcolm Claud had no idea that Abu subconsciously considered himself by far the superior being. Claud made the cardinal mistake of thinking that no newspaper in Dubai could run without his expertise. He was, after all, the 'great white father' of the *Gulf News*. He had already let slip the interesting fact that Jim Headgear was no editor at all. 'The closest he's been to a newspaper is to put a dressing gown over his jammies and go to the landing to collect the *Mirror*,' he said. And then he would say with some complacence, 'Don't any of you forget it. I'm the hot shot here and what I say goes.'

We decided otherwise. The 23rd was fast approaching and Claud had made no indication that there would be a *Gulf News*. Abu was getting worried. Claud had his own escape route planned.

'I cannot produce a newspaper with a bunch of incompetent Sri Lankans,' he said. He was obviously missing his crew of wangers who had wrecked the newspaper in the first place. Having to kow-tow with Asians went much against his grain. There was some talk about re-arranging his face but this was frowned on.

Eventually matters came to a head. With the finesse of a very block-headed bull in the main outlet of a china shop, Claud marched upon Abu with the breathless news that the paper should be recalled to life on, say, 23 December. Abu hit the roof. He had, he said, lost a lot of sympathy for ginger moustaches. Also, he was mathematically competent enough to know that he would have to sit and watch his staff lounging around and making innumerable trips to the coffee dispenser while he was bereft of earnings.

Jim Headgear was of no help either. He said that while he was the Editor, the actual working (and non-working) of the paper lay squarely on the shoulders of Malcolm Claud.

Abu cut through the flab. 'Can you produce a paper on 23 March?' he asked.

'We-ell . . . ' said Jim Headgear.

'No!' said Claud.

'You're fired!'

Just like that. We had no idea of the high drama that was going on behind the curtains of Abu's office. Claud came into the newsroom looking like a Sunday picnicker on the Thames who had been hit, bows on, by the QE2.

'Hullo,' said Nihal Kaneira, 'something's up.'

Claud dived into his little cubby hole and came out with a briefcase. 'The British gave civilization to half the world,' he intoned, 'but the bleeding wogs will have their way!' and with this ha' p'orth of wisdom, he stalked out.

'What was all that in aid of?' asked Dudley Fernando of no one in particular.

I shrugged. Then D.B. Suranimala, the Sri Lankan General Manager, was summoned to Abu's office. When he popped in, Jim Headgear popped out. 'This,' I told G.W. Surendra, 'is getting interesting.'

Jim was a nice enough guy. Naturally, he laboured under the delusion that with no Englishman at the helm there could be no *Gulf News*. He came to us, ahemmed twice.

'I have to apologize,' he said, 'for bringing you chaps here. Claud has resigned. He will not be coming here any more and will fly out soon. I advised Abu not to accept his resignation but these people don't seem to understand how a newspaper is run. Anyway, without Claud, I see no reason to go on either. I have also quit. I have told Abu to be as fair as possible with you. He will pay your wages for

this month and there should be another month's pay
added on and the tickets to go back. I'm sure you will all
be sent home as soon as he can arrange things.' He sighed
and shrugged his shoulders. 'Well, life is full of little
surprises, isn't it? It's been nice knowing you.'

Then D. B. Suranimala poked a head out and we were
summoned to the sanctum. Headgear watched us go with
a beatific 'I told you so' expression. If he had a rifle, he
may have presented arms.

The old time nomads of the Arabian desert developed
a strong religious tradition. Supreme God is Allah, and
this all-knowing, all-powerful and all-wise God has the
power to change what has been set forth by man. This
gave the Arab a fatalism which is deeply ingrained in the
Bedouin character.

One could consider how a powerful and mystical
sense of kinship could be built among a people who used
to wander back and forth in a harsh and unforgiving
desert environment. This kinship was overlaid by attitudes
of natural superiority and a deep fatalism. It engendered
in the Arab nature a singular type of heroism. Heroic
deeds were constantly executed, if only to combat the
monotony of desert existence. This heroism is constantly
brought to the surface as the modern Arab enters the
modern world. The heroics of spending his new oil wealth
has made the Arab a legend of our times.

When entering Abu's office I thought: 'What happens
now depends on this man's attitude.' But I substituted
*attitude* for *heroism*. He just looked at us and asked one
question: 'Can you produce a newspaper on March 23rd?'

I said yes. Loud and clear.

'Good. Then go and do so.'

D.B. Suranimala led us into his office. 'I know you

guys can do it,' he said, 'so give it your best shot.' We fixed our several duties and sauntered back to the newsroom where Jim Headgear was packing.

'That was quick,' he said.

'Yes,' I said, 'pity you won't be here to read the *Gulf News* on 23 March.'

He stared. No, goggled. He heard us out. Then he laughed: 'Well . . . I don't know what to say. I knew I had chosen well in Sri Lanka.' We parted on the best of terms. Later, he wrote us from London. He had become a Public Relations Officer . . . for a brewery!

We consoled ourselves that the *Gulf News* was a tabloid and, with the best will in the world, could be produced with reasonable dispatch. But there was much to learn. Besides the intricacies of computerized setting which was a bane to the traditional 'hot metal' sub-editors, there were the other niceties and complexities of writing in the Middle East. There was, for one thing, no such body of water as the Persian Gulf. There were the waters of the Arabs and thus, were the Arabian Gulf!

It was said that the Shah of Iran's lips would curl up in disdain when the word 'Arab' was mentioned. 'A patch of sand,' he once said, referring to the UAE. 'In twenty years all the oil will be finished and then what?' The Shah's attitude was that the UAE and other Gulf States had a great deal to gain from accepting Iran as a 'big brother'.

'They treat us with much unfairness,' he once told a reporter. 'We help them on the international scene and include them in our declarations in the UN. We do a lot for them behind the scenes. What do they do? They declare the Persian Gulf is the Arabian Gulf!'

We were soon to learn that lots of things were quite unpalatable and politically unpardonable in print. The taboos were legion. Hassan Al Bana, founder of the Muslim Brotherhood, had declared that the ideologies of the West had to be resisted. 'They are the forward arm of corruption,' he had declared, 'the silken curtain·behind which hides the greed of graspers and the dreams of the dominators!'

The Gulf tries to resist . . . and one form is censorship. The problem is that no one really knew how far up the road one could travel. The London *Financial Times* was banned once for suggesting that the rulers of Saudi Arabia and Kuwait were elderly and not in good health. When a Lebanese friend of mine tried to translate Shakespeare's *A Midsummer Night's Dream* he was told to bring the author for interview to the Ministry of Cultural Affairs!

Censorship is everywhere. Nudity is taboo. The backroom boys in the Customs office have a whale of a time with black felt-tipped pens, blacking out boobs and bums with carefree abandon. Even Michelangelo's Sistine Chapel paintings, once reproduced in a German magazine, were blotted out. British newspapers get the full treatment.

As journalists, we had to watch out for anything that, in the wildest stretch of imagination, could be thought anti- or un-Islamic. Letting any such get through could mean the certain death of the paper and its staff would be frog-marched to the airport at two in the morning!

Ticker news from agencies also had to be carefully vetted. Even crime stories had to be carefully considered and vetted for it used to be a matter of national pride at that time to declare the country crime-free.

Then, there was the constant confusion over titles. Who was a Sheikh and who was not? Tribal and family names had to be spot on because there was a fierce desert pride in every aspect of Arab life. Tribal traditions, competition and oft-times jealousy remain powerful emotional forces in the Gulf to this day.

Nihal Kaneira and Lateef Farouk had to go through a sort of baptism of fire. They were the reporters in our party. Oh, there was plenty going on, both openly and covertly, but nothing one could write about. The safest bet was the entertainment scene:

SHERATON PLANS DISNEYLAND BUFFET . . .
PERRY COMO TO SING AT THE HILTON . . .
STRAWBERRY FESTIVAL AT DUBAI INTERNATIONAL HOTEL . . .

Or one could write paens of praise on the glorious gallop of the UAE into the 21st century:

JEBEL ALI WILL BE MIDDLE EAST'S LARGEST PORT . . .
ABU DHABI GIVES GREEN LIGHT FOR SECOND AIRPORT . . .
UAE IS RESPECTED VOICE ON WORLD SCENE . . .

Leader writers must be quick to comment on the amazing progress of the country and hail the farsightedness and benevolence of the rulers. 'Just go along with it,' was our credo. 'We are not here to shape the country—just to milk it a little!'

With all this to consider, we got down to the serious business of bringing the *Gulf News* back into circulation. Several pages were pasted up and locked away on the 22nd. We tortured the computers with our trial and error methods of sub-editing which gave us headlines like this:

B e rli n
orchestra to
tour U A E

Gopalakrishnan was our Indian computer operator. 'What is this, brother,' he would wail, 'you did not code left your headline, no?'

'So go and code left the bloody thing!'

He would go away, sniffing.

At 11.45 p.m. on 22 March 1979, only the front page waited for anything that had to be rushed in. The paper was ready. Like the blind leading the blind, we had hung on to each other, pooled mind and muscle to bring a national newspaper back to life. There was no editor. Just a crazy bunch of journalists.

Proud? No. Too damn tired! The presses rolled at one a.m. Dudley Fernando drank his twenty-third cup of coffee and stood up.

'Where are you going?'

'Home.'

'Sit down. We have tomorrow's paper to think about . . . now!'

Claud poked his head in. He was on his way to the airport. There was a decided sag in his face.

Exit God . . . and all was right with the world of the *Gulf News!*

*Oh The
Manners . . . Oh
The Customs*

Fly with me, and all your sins declare,
And if you're overburdened, say a prayer!

'This is your captain speaking. Delhi airport authorities require that the cabins of this aircraft be deodorized before landing. We will now commence to spray the cabins. You may close your eyes briefly to avoid any discomfort.'

Let us spray . . .

I was treated to the sight of a little cabin attendant running up and down the aisles, coat flapping, clutching an aerosol in his upraised hand. Like the last of the Valkyries. He hissed as he ran. No. It was the can that hissed. A belligerent goose of a can. The aircraft began to smell like the loo of a five-star hotel. I looked out of the window. Dawn over Delhi was not a pretty sight. The country below the wingtip was like a dirty dishcloth. The sunlight danced on the turboprop. Inside, the stench of lemon and cut limes was overpowering.

We landed with a thud. Coasting the tarmac was like riding the noon stage into Dakota. Even the seat-belt juddered the diaphragm. I was not heavy laden. Just a beat-up suitcase, briefcase and camera. I walked into a sea of humanity that, at five-thirty in the morning, was positively unnerving.

If anything raises eyebrows at an airport, it is my passport. It looks like the old, oily pocketbook of a bazaar trader in Khota Baru. The Sri Lanka government had

101

issued me this passport upon whose black cover were the words PASSPORT—DEMOCRATIC SOCIALIST REPUBLIC OF SRI LANKA in letters of gold. Yes, gold. But the gold had come off long ago.

'What's this?'

'Passport.'

I get a keen look. The kind of look that says, 'I've seen passports and passports.' I look past the immigration officer's shoulder. He studies each page doubtfully. The Indian visa reassures him. 'Go to Baggage,' he says.

Easier said than done. Where the devil is Baggage? There's baggage everywhere. Indians, I'll have you know, don't travel light. After shuddering over hundreds of heaps of suitcases, boxes, bales of stuff wrapped and hog-tied with straw matting and canvas, I begin to lose orientation. One doesn't go to Baggage . . . . The whole damn airport is Baggage. You just pick your spot and wallow.

The bag tracks keep up their perpetual motion. People cluster around, mesmerized. I lean against a mountain of crates. From somewhere, I tell myself, my suitcase will emerge. It did, and it came forth so ill-used and wan, I could hardly recognize it. All the spirit had been beaten out of it. Like a dry birth plus forceps. I rescued it from the carousel on its second orbit and lugged it to Customs.

'I will be taking back my camera,' I said.

'Ah, it is your camera?'

'Of course it is.'

'Achcha . . . then you must declare for re-export.'

'I declare.' Should I tell him I'm for re-export too. No, he will not be amused. It was too early in the morning.

'You have anything else to declare?'

I shook my head.

'No dutiable articles?'

'No.'

'Where you are staying in Delhi?'

'Ashok Hotel.'

'Good. You go now and declare your camera that you're taking back.'

It was the beginning of a saga.

The line of people who brought in dutiable articles to sell but declared them for re-export in order to avoid paying Customs duty was the longest I had ever seen in any airport. I stood. There was little else to do. A man with a fierce moustache and bleary eyes stood behind a low counter. He eyed us with loathing. He must have been up since midnight, judging by the bags under each eye. The operation, I noted, was a bureaucratic idea of Limbo. There were forms to fill and chops to chop, stamps to slap on, cross references to get cross-eyed over and squiggles to make. The man behind the counter would pause, suck the top of his Biro, look painfully down the line and mentally consign us all to some special place of torment in ancient Hindu mythology. He would then examine the top of his Biro, possibly checking for erosion, then return to his task. At length I thrust my camera under his nose and proferred my passport.

'You're going back when? Ticket?'

Shown.

'You're taking back camera?'

I nodded.

'Why?'

'It's mine.'

'Ah,' he scribbled furiously. He looked at his Biro again, decided against taking a nibble and put it down with a sigh. 'What is the value?'

He had me there. The camera was pretty old. Older,

by far, than my suitcase. It had ingested its fair share of dust and grit. It was also a sort of merger of three photographic companies—one for the camera, one for the lens and another for the flash. It was a hybrid of the worst sort for a red-eyed Delhian.

'Make is Mamiya,' he said unnecessarily.

I nodded.

He wrote 'Mamiya' laboriously. 'What is number?'

'Search me.'

'You have anything else?'

'No . . . what?' I was confused.

'Then for what for I must search you?'

I decided to button up. We were getting nowhere.

'You not know the number, ah?'

'No.'

He perked up. A new challenge had been thrown at him at seven in the morning. I longed for a cup of tea.

'Lens have number,' he informed no one in particular. He wrote that down carefully. He gave the camera the once over. 'Ah, have number for flash.' This was also written down with a flourish. Good, I thought, we are getting along. The camera proper was given the third degree. 'No number,' he said mournfully.

'What do you mean? There must be a number.'

'I have looked. Here, you look.' ·

'How you can bring a camera with no any number?' asks the man behind me. 'My God, now will have to stand behind you for all the day.'

I ignored him. Greater things were at stake. I was in possession of a piece of equipment unheard of in the annals of Delhi Customs. The camera was cannibalized with a concentration awesome to behold. The lens was removed and held up to the admiring gaze of other Customs wallahs who had gathered round to see duty done. A roll of film was extracted and placed on the counter with the reverence usually reserved for the Dead Sea Scrolls. 'You see,' I was informed in a hushed voice, 'inside, outside, frontside, backside, nothing. No number.'

'That's bad?'

'Is very bad. I must enter number of camera, no?'

'Perhaps,' I said brightly, 'the lens number is also for the camera.'

'Must be sample camera,' put in one of the Customs onlookers.

Appealing thought. I had this sinking feeling that my camera did have a number, originally. A sort of etched or raised serial which, through years of usage and roughage, had been obliterated. Telling that to Delhi Customs was not going to help. It might even complicate matters.

It was now creeping on to eight-fifteen. I have been in New Delhi for two hours and forty-five minutes and had advanced no more than eight hundred yards into Indian territory. Wonder what Clive would have done. Up in the gallery, behind glass panels, my host was having hysterics. The poor man had rolled out of bed at five in the morning to welcome me. I stood. He stood.

The Customs men went into a huddle. A sort of mini summit. They looked at me on occasion. One frowned. Another grinned. They examined my passport as if it were the Grimoire of Honorius. They scratched their heads. Then they all beetled off to an office and returned with a Big Brass who had several clusters of what looked like silver-plated gooseberries on his epaulettes. He was a cheery soul.

'So you have camera without number? Ha, ha, must be stolen property, no?'

'Tis the season to be jolly!

'You're taking it back, no?'

'That's why I've been here from six in the morning.'

'Ha, ha, you should have told us that camera haven't any number.'

The man behind me agreed vehemently. 'I am standing and standing,' he moaned.

'I'll tell you what? You take camera and go. We will enter that it is a prototype.'

'That's fine,' I said. Suddenly there was light at the end of the storm drain. The officer sucked his Biro meditatively. He wrote 'camera' but he drew the line at 'prototype'. It seemed that the whole affair had gone beyond his ken. He had never entered 'prototype' before and he was not going to set a precedent now. Besides, how the devil do you spell 'prototype'?

I walked stiffly to the barrier where my host told me that even the garland of frangipani he had intended to hang around my neck had wilted. 'What was wrong?' he asked.

I shot him a dirty look. 'First tea,' I said.

It was ten minutes to nine. Delhi was wide awake. Scootershaws whizzed by and crows were scolding raucously. The air was as crisp as early lettuce.

I had arrived.

# Seventy Millimetres
# Of Trouble

Bagged and bussed! These humans take the cake!
Am I not, then, a self-respecting snake?

Herbert Zilva called it *Echis carinata*. 'It's a viperine,' he said, 'and bad-tempered too. Thanks, anyway. I've been looking for a specimen. Never thought of the seashore.'[*]

He then tried to transfer said Echis into a glass and cement tank and was bitten. But he got the pale, russet serpent into the tank, secured it and gave me a look of dumb accusation. 'Now look what you've done,' he grumbled. 'I'm going to be sick for days.'

'You're not going to die, are you?' I asked faintly.

'Worse,' he snarled, 'these snakes take the pith out of you. The poison is going to sap me. Go away. I'm going to put some ginger paste on this,' indicating three fang marks on the inside of his wrist.

I didn't go away. I was concerned, naturally. Herbie was a herpetologist. He studied snakes, collected them, did all manner of fearless things with them and accepted that they would, sooner or later, put the bite on him.

'What do you feel?' I asked.

It was like an electric shock, he said, racing from wrist to neck and all along the right side of his body. 'Pulse is rapid,' he muttered, smearing the bite with ginger paste. A few drops of blood had oozed out of the bite. I fussed

---

[*]    The events of this story first appeared in *The Python of Pura Malai and Other Stories* (Puffin, 1995).

behind him like a mother hen. The pain from the bite was getting worse and stung like billy-oh. In half an hour his hand had begun to swell. 'There's nothing you can do,' he gritted. 'I'm going to sit on that bench. I'm going to suffer. You happy?'

Assured for the fourth time that he was not going to die, I went home. Uneasily. Echis had moved with incredible speed. In the plastic bag it had coiled itself into a ball and kept writhing its body continuously. The sound of its pectinate scales grating against each other had turned the bus into a mobile ward in Bedlam. I thought of the irate conductor, the panicking passengers and of how we had been shooed off a long way from our destination, and chuckled.

'You gave Herbie the snake?' my wife asked.

'Yes.'

'He liked it?'

'I think so. It bit him.'

'Oh.'

It had been quite an evening. We, my wife and I, had gone for a stroll along the beach: the sort of thing married couples indulge in from time to time. Above the belt of yellow sand was a dingier stretch of white, gritty sand, carpeted with a leathery, butterfly-leaved creeper that spread as far as the eye could see. Nice evening. The wind had gentled and the waves were long, effortless ripples that seemed to seep out of the purpling reef and the gold red glow of a lowering sun. The sands were a hive of activity. Tiny crabs scuttled hither and thither while their hermit cousins waggled stubby legs out of shells like telegraphists morse-coding the limpets on the weed-strewn rocks. Gulls wheeled overhead, greedily seeking an evening meal.

We were picking our way across the carpet of green when I spotted Echis. At the time I didn't know just what it was. Seventy millimetres of pale russet and brown and olive-yellow with ochre and dun markings in broad arrow shapes. Certainly a viper. In Trincomalee I had met the Russel's brand, roaming the beaches at dusk, hunting hermit crabs. This had to be a viper of sorts. Not like anything I had seen before.

'What is it?' my wife asked, and naturally. 'Is it dangerous?'

Ignorance, authority expounds, is bliss. If I had known what sort of vicious creature I intended tangling with, I would have decided against being a damn fool and put a lot of beach between us. But I thought: 'Herbie will like this fellow,' and closed in. Echis was oozing its way through the tough roots and leathery leaves. I casually grabbed at its tail. It tried to do its ball-of-wool act, but a lot of its seventy millimetres was in the spreading root frame and it only tangled itself up, although it did manage to fix an eye on me after turning its short, snouted head. 'This, my lad, won't do,' it seemed to say.

The idea is that the snake will always try to head directly away from where its tail is. I then grab it by its constricted neck and lift it up, a captive. I flicked sand at it, and Echis must have decided that here was a lunatic of sorts. People usually left it alone. Moreso, they left it period! It would have me know that it had two fangs on each maxillary. That's how much of VIP it was. What was I? Some kind of a nut?

It lowered its head, stretched, tried to launch itself out of the creeper and I had it. Boy, it was gritty. And even with its mouth opening threateningly as I held it fast, it refused to hiss. Strong silent type!

'So what do we do now?' my wife asked. Always the practical soul, she pointed out that we were on a beach where no containers to accommodate members of the reptile world were available. Echis had coiled around my forearm and was very annoyed.

'Come on,' I said, 'we'll borrow a plastic bag. Herbie must have this beauty.'

We crossed the coastal railtrack, went up a lane and tapped on the door of a house. A lady in an atrocious housecoat emerged and glared at us suspiciously. I explained the urgent need for a plastic bag or container. She said she would look. Soon, a little servant boy came out with an assortment of bags. 'Lady said to take,' he said with a sniff. Then, seeing Echis, he gave a whoop and bolted. I selected a bag, unravelled the snake from my forearm and slipped it in. I didn't know how fast it was, but it sure looked mean. It was turning like a jet fighter, primed for attack, when the bag was nipped shut, twisted twice and knotted at the neck. Housecoat watched from a window with full moon eyes. 'What is that thing?' she screeched. 'Take it away at once, do you hear?' We did just that.

'Well,' I said, 'some people are the limit.'

My wife agreed. 'And you're Abou Ben Adhem.'

'And who the devil is he?'

'Some old fellow I read about. He led all the rest.'

Ha, ha!

Plans change. Circs alter cases. Our evening excursion was intended to be one of life's quiet pleasures. Savour the sunset, wallow in the beauty of a golden beach, see the clouds catch the sunfire and observe twilight's last gleaming. The viperine changed all that. What was now of the essence was to catch the first bus home. A simple manoeuvre, where one ambles to the bus stop, boards a crowded belching behemoth with a conductor who rattles more than the motor and be jerked out of one's skin if not squashed flat. It had its native charm, of course, but an action not to be recommended to the weak, the aged and mothers-to-be.

Sri Lanka's buses have front and rear doors . . . generally. We took a rear seat and crammed into it. Echis in its plastic home, was convulsed in fury. The top of the bag was clouded as it breathed hard and kept spitting venomously. It had balled up and kept up an infernal *scrish-scrish*, like someone surreptitiously scratching his backside. To say that the bus was crowded would be to put it very mildly. The inside of every bus looks like an image from Dante. People hang on in every conceivable angle, twisted bodies, tortured faces, shoulder to shoulder, back to back, jostling, trampling, sweating, swearing, while body odours rise like some fearsome cloud. The poor man's Benz, we call our buses. In transit, said poor man will benz this way and benz that way, finally fighting his way out at his destination to walk home like a pretzel in a hurricane.

Even as we sat, hordes of humans literally hung over us. They clung on grimly, arching backs and hips, some doubled up in defeat, others using elbows to prod ribs, groins, eyes, that swam into their space. I hung onto my bag with a deepening frown. Every time the viperine took a deep, indignant breath, the bag would deflate, then inflate, and the struggle within was unrelenting.

'If that thing gets free . . .' my wife hissed.

'Don't even think of it,' I muttered.

A man, arched over us at such an angle that we couldn't actually determine where he stood, was staring at the bag. He gave me a knowing smile. 'Rubber toy snake, no?'

I wished to God it was. His remark drew the attention of others jammed around. I nodded weakly. The man leaned over until I thought he would give way in the middle. Just then Echis went into his routine of coiling, arching and scrishing madly. The man shot back in alarm. 'How he did that!' he yelped. 'That is a real snake!'

Ever tried yelling 'snake' in a crowded bus? The cry is taken up like a national anthem. The aisle became a torrent of higgledy-piggledy arms and legs snarling up each other. Someone shouted 'Naya!' (cobra) and a high-pitched woman carolled 'Pambu!' (snake—never mind what, but a snake!). Some stamped, destroyed other's corns and demanded 'where? where?' while others pointed at the conductor and shouted 'there! there!' Everybody, apparently, shared the same burning desire: to put as much distance as possible between the snake and themselves, and soon the whole boiling were standing or perched on the seats, shouting 'Snake!' in forty different sharps and flats. The driver brought the vehicle to a shuddering stop. Order was restored with some difficulty and ere long, every baleful eye homed in on the bag I carried.

'Out! Out! Out!' the conductor fumed. 'You mad persons, no? How you can carry snakes in bus? This is people bus!'

We nipped out. As we rose, there was a stampede for the front door. We walked home in dignified silence.

'Cheer up,' the wife said. 'Think of all the tales those people will tell when they get home.'

I grinned at the thought, and while my wife turned for home, I went to Herbie's . . . and so we come to the beginning of this story.

Herbie was like Mr Michelin when I called the next day. The swelling was intense and he moaned that the stinging pain around the bite was severe. He had difficulty in walking, had stabbing pains in his head and could not sleep because of a burning sensation in his eyes. Also, he declared, he was feeling chilly. He was preparing a foul looking paste. 'It's a compound used by local snake-bite doctors,' he explained. 'This should do the trick.'

It took six months to full recovery and he became very emaciated in the process. I would consider Echis in its tank with respect. Seventy millimetres of pure trouble. It was quite at home. Herbie kept it well supplied with frogs, lizards and baby rats as well as a mixed salad of insects including centipedes and scorpions. But it was as mean tempered as ever.

As Herbie said, it can really knock the stuffing out of you. Sobering thought. It's strictly seashells on the seashore now!

# The Unhinging Of
# Hillocks

> An empty mug on a dead man's chest,
> Yo! Ho! Ho! and a bottle of booze,
> Drink and the devil will do for the rest,
> Yo! Ho! Ho! till you lose your screws!

If the Commanding Officer of Her Majesty's Ceylon Shore Establishment Elara hadn't been so all-fired anxious to get rid of Able Seaman Abey, nothing would have happened. Abey was dead, true, but upon receiving the news and the medical report, Navy Headquarters in Colombo had informed the dead seaman's family who acknowledged that they would go to Talaimannar and collect the body.

But our C.O. was in a hurry. He found a dead Abey a bigger nuisance than a live one. Also, the man had died of typhoid and someone had told him that germs don't hang around a man after he dies. They go looking for other bodies to infest. They are a determined lot, and typhoid germs are the worst. They like to make you very sick and then kill you.

A grieving party of parents and relations were put out to learn that the corpse had been placed in a coffin, the box artfully draped with a naval White Ensign and thereupon dispatched to Colombo in a five-ton Navy truck. 'I told that stoker to drive slowly,' the C.O. told the bereaved, who complained that they had done a long journey for nothing. 'And we brought a coffin also. Now we have to take it and go back to Colombo.'

The C.O. invited them to stay to lunch and Abey's mother threw a tantrum and smote her forehead and shook loose her hair and became most tragic. A large glass of mango juice calmed her down and the C.O. organized a work party to book seats on the night's mail train to Colombo and escort the family to the beach and show them around the neighbourhood. This, too, had its bits and pieces of drama since one of Abey's uncles disappeared and was later found in the toddy tavern, hiccoughing rudely.

It must also be said that Stoker Mechanic Arnold drove Abey to Colombo at top speed. With long, empty roads, and jungle-fringed at that, and feeling most perturbed that Abey was behind him and very dead, he stood on the accelerator. He did squash a few goats, but as he later said, he stopped taking count. All he wanted was to get Abey out of his truck as quickly as possible.

Lieutenant Commander Ingle Darling was annoyed. The C.O. of Elara had been told to hang on to Abey. Maybe signals had crossed as they always most annoyingly did, but he hadn't expected a mad-looking Stoker who had roared up to the gates, hopped out of a dust-creamed truck, barged in and said: 'Get that dead bugger out. From Elara I'm coming.' Ingleton was even more put out when another signal was brought to him. It said that AB Abey's funeral party was leaving Talaimannar that night and would take over the body in Colombo. Hold, it said, corpse for collection.

So, after a lot of shouting and lots of 'fucks' (which is standard Naval procedure) Abey was carried to the Armoury and a space cleared among the rifle racks, the boxes of cartridges and the piles of steel helmets.

'We've got to keep him on something. Here you, pile

those boxes of cartridges together. That's right, make a platform,' the Duty Petty Officer ordered, and Abey was finally dumped on a big bier of wooden boxes on each of which was stencilled in red: 303 CLIPS 2000 and a big X.

'Can't keep him unattended. Go and tell the quartermaster to post a guard. Two men. Four hour watches.'

Stoker Mechanic Arnold drank his third bottle of beer in the Canteen. He said that driving from Talaimannar (which is in the north-east of the island) makes a man very, very thirsty. Also, he had come over 300 miles with a dead body and had left Talaimannar at five in the morning and it was now two in the afternoon and he intended to drink until the reasonable hour of ten and then collapse. He had earned it, he declared.

The Navy has this system of Watches. A sailor on shore is given a rifle and told to conduct a routine guard duty for a four-hour watch. Two sailors, actually, in the case of Abey, since the duty P.O. thought it only correct that two men watch over the corpse. Also, in the quartermaster's lobby someone had said: 'Hell, I'm not going anywhere near that bloody armoury with that dead body in there. Not in the bloody night anyway.' So, for the eight to midnight watch two of Her Majesty's Ceylon Ship *Gemunu's* biggest and rowdiest seamen were detailed—Able Seaman Koelmeyer and Stoker Mechanic Tucker. That too was a mistake. It made Stoker Mechanic Hillocks mad. *Real* mad, like bonkers, loco, crazy, loony. *That* sort of mad!

Tucker and Koelmeyer were inseparables. They had two goals in life: sex and booze . . . and they were also inseparable in both pursuits. They picked up women on the strict understanding that the woman would do for one what she would do for the other. If they ever argued, it

121

was about who should be first and when a coin had been finally flipped, one would stand over and watch the other perform, while the other would tell the bemused woman, 'Anything I fuck he also fucks!' In the Navy, one would not think of one without the other. Like Laurel and Hardy. Or David and Goliath. They were in the same Blue Watch and got into trouble together and were punished together. This time, they slung rifles on their shoulders and went to the Armoury. Together, they would guard Abey, from 8 p.m. to midnight. Stoker Mechanic Hillocks and I would relieve them. We had the graveyard watch—from midnight to 4 a.m.

At midnight I yawned hugely and blinked my way to the quartermaster's lobby. Hillocks was already there. A little fellow with no conversation, he would be a dreary companion for four dreary hours.

'Who's there now?' he asked.

'Tucker and Koelmeyer,' the QM said, 'but if I know those buggers, they would have gone off by now. Anyway, you guys get going. It's past twelve.'

'You go ahead,' I told Hillocks as I watched the kettle. 'I'll bring a pot of tea.'

'Fine. Bring a mug also,' Hillocks reminded and dragged off down the road to the end of Flagstaff Street where the Armoury was. It took me all of ten minutes to make the tea and cadge a tin mug. Very sweet tea. Keeps one up, especially when the minutes drag by as though they were stuck up to the ears in chewing gum.

I didn't see Tucker or Koelmeyer. I should have met them since they had to report end of watch to the QM, but plainly, such procedures meant little to them. Chances were that they had just slung their rifles and drifted down road to the port where sundry daughters of the night roamed for custom. Tucker and Koelmeyer always bundled in one of these women after a night watch. For some time, however, they had been quite restrained—ever since the night that they had brought in a hermaphrodite and discovered that their prize had a penis! The ensuing hullaballoo had been quite extraordinary!

I changed my mind when on approaching the Armoury, I heard a voice. But no, it was Hillocks. The man was speaking. At the door I paused. It was Hillocks, to be sure, and he was inside the armoury and his voice was edged with pure terror. 'Don't you try to get up! Don't! You get up you bastard I'll shoot you! I will! Lie down! Did you hear! Don't try to get up! Don't try to get up! I'll shoot! I'll shoot you!'

I rushed in with a clatter and Hillocks wailed and swung the rifle, blindly squeezing the trigger. It wasn't loaded, of course, and I dropped the kettle and grabbed at him, receiving a stinging blow as he swung the barrel. He was white, drenched in sweat, utterly ghastly. He hung grimly to his weapon, finger hooked under the trigger guard, and he drooled, yes, actually drooled.

Dropping my rifle I wrenched at his weapon, pulling it free and almost breaking his finger. He screamed and rushed at me, making for the door and turning his ankle on the kettle, falling heavily. I grabbed a leg and hung on. The man was trying to swim for the road! There was no help for it. I dragged him back, and leaning over punched him hard on the back of his neck. He subsided, whimpering.

I had not really taken note of the armoury. Satisfied that Hillocks would behave I looked around and nearly jumped out of my skin. There was the coffin. The flag lay on the floor. The coffin lid had been removed. Actually the lid had not been screwed down. Awaiting the arrival of the family it had been merely laid in place and the flag draped over it. Even Stoker Mechanic Arnold, when later informed of this, was most indignant. 'You mean I brought that bugger all the way and the box was open? My God, the speed I was coming, could have bounced out and fallen on the road also and I wouldn't have known!' He said his faith in the Navy was shattered.

Abey, dead and stiff, was not a pretty sight. Furthermore he had not stayed in the confines of his coffin. He was practically half way out, entire head, shoulders and midriff, and on his chest was a tin mug, and on the floor an empty arrack bottle. Tucker and Koelmeyer had had a party. And, being congenial souls, invited Abey to it.

At the subsequent inquiry it was grudgingly admitted that the two incorrigibles had gone to their duty with a bottle of hooch and a mug. In the armoury they had settled down to finish the bottle and midway, had decided to toast the corpse.

'Oi, Abey, you're acksherlly dead? What the 'ell . . . how 'bout a small drink?'

'Thash true. Not good we are only drinkin' and 'e's jus' lyin' there.'

'Sho—sho givimm also a drink.'

'I say, pukka—puk-kah idea. Oi, Abey, you wanter drink?'

'Don' know what 'e's sayin' inside that bloody coffin.'

'Sho open men—opennit!'

They dragged off the flag, found a lid that moved and yanked it off.

'Bugger is dead? How to put a drink when he's shleep—shleepin' like that? Oi, Abey—Arrbey! Gettup, you ole bugger. Have sum arrack you want?'

'Nottin doin', bugger won't budge. Here, cumman 'elp make him sit.'

Together they had tried to raise the corpse and succeeded in dragging him halfway out of the box and he must have looked most peculiar, poker stiff and all.

'If iffyew don' dont wan' to drink just say,' said Koelmeyer, getting peeved. 'Now becos 'e's dead must be thinkin' he can't put a shot.'

'Balls,' said Tucker, pouring the last of the arrack into the mug. He swallowed a great mouthful and gave the rest to Koelmeyer who tossed it down. With some effort, they managed to place the empty mug on Abey's chest. 'When 'e gets the smell he'll quickly get up an' ask.'

Koelmeyer wagged a finger at the corpse. 'An' when you arshk you won' get. Bottle finished. Let the bugger be. Come go!'

'Where?'

'Go an' shleep. Dam' shleepy now. See the way 'e's sleepin'.'

Tucker had some of his senses intact. 'But not yet twelve.'

'Sho? Wait an' do what? Come go!'

They had left the armoury at twenty minutes to midnight. Hillocks, coming in, had flipped. There was the dead man, head and shoulders out of the coffin, a mug on his chest, an empty bottle on the floor. He refused to be convinced. 'He's alive!' he howled. 'And have been drinking also. See the mug!' The poor man was trembling. I tried to make him stand but he preferred to crawl. He was bathed in sweat and made queer noises in his throat. There was nothing else to do. Hauling him up, dragging him along while he sagged horribly, I made painful progress to the sick bay. Hillocks was in a bad way. The sick bay attendant said he had a high fever and pushed him into a bed where he would lie quiet, trembling, gasping, then suddenly break into a howl and try to bunk out of the window. Eventually he was strapped down, an icebag placed on his head and, on the advice of the duty petty officer, a deck shoe jammed into his mouth the next time he tried to blast off. It was shock, of course, and he was in near delirium and took a full three days to get sensible.

Abey was pushed back and a shipwright summoned to fasten the coffin lid and make things shipshape. Tucker and Koelmeyer were brought on defaulters parade and grinned throughout the proceedings. It was decided to send them to sea with the pious wish that they would get sozzled and fall overboard. Hillocks was recommended a change of air and within a month, was drafted to Talaimannar where he, too, contacted typhoid and was dispatched to the Mannar hospital. There, Catholic nursing sisters took him to their bosoms and gave him a Bible and read the Scriptures to him and he listened and wept and did not die and got stranger with each passing day. There was no hope for the poor guy. He was clearly round the bend.

It was thought that the sea would put him right. He was drafted on board the HMCyS *Vijaya*, a minesweeper, but this, too, was a mistake. He was in that nice little state between lunatic and fanatic. The nuns of Mannar had steeped him in religion. But he also believed that the dead do rise to steep themselves in booze. Something had to give. When he appeared on deck in long green pyjamas and wanted to preach to the ship's company on Sundays, skipper Victor Hunter decided that the man should go. I was Captain's secretary. Hunter twirled a finger and told me to draft a signal. Hillocks had to be committed. He was taken ashore at Trincomalee where an ambulance awaited. He gave us a solemn blessing and went away,

Bible in one hand and a packet of ginger snaps in the other.

A month or so later I told Koelmeyer and Tucker: 'You buggers are happy? You put Hillocks in the asylum.'

Koelmeyer closed one eye. He had reached the stage where he was seeing double. 'Bollocks!' he said.

'Not bollocks! Hillocks!'

'So? What's the difference? Bollocks, Hillocks, all mad buggers here anyway . . . '

# The New God Of The Gulf

> Ready Cash is now enthroned,
> Greed and Waste his pages,
> Strutting through the lands of oil,
> Mocking leaner ages

Islam does not accept that it is more difficult for a rich man to enter the kingdom of heaven than for a camel to get through the eye of a needle. Why all this Christian prudishness about money?

The Arabs had created an empire that was larger than ancient Rome. They conquered half the civilized world in those days of yore. Yet, for centuries into the modern age, they were ignored and humiliated and defeated by the infidel. Now, this same infidel queued up to worship the God everyone is ready to believe in: Cash!

When a journalist in the Gulf, I interviewed the Saudi Minister for Industry who had come to Bahrain to discuss the proposed Bahrain-Saudi causeway.

'Money?' he said. 'Ah, it is really a curious experience having all this money. Suddenly, because of this thing which is oil, we have become a world power. This oil is neither permanent nor really important. But the money allows us to achieve in a short time what it has taken the West centuries to achieve.'

Always, the Arab insists, religion gets pride of place. Banks are bought, businesses are bought, property in the US, UK, Europe and Japan is bought, and while enmeshed

131

in the throes of mergers, deals and counterdeals, the Arab will lavish his wealth on the building of luxuriously appointed mosques and conduct a sort of international *zakat*—charity to developing nations—to maintain the image that he is the world's most reasonable creature, the soul of generosity and fount of goodwill.

In fact, the Abu Dhabi Fund for Arab Development has as its motto: 'We have not forgotten our poverty; now we shall share our wealth.'

Nothing was sacred to the Arab with money. As newsmen, we laughed when we heard that a Saudi businessman wanted to buy the Alamo for his son as a birthday gift, but it didn't stop there. The Arab League once discussed the advisability of taking over *The Times* and there have been perfectly serious Arab inquiries towards the purchase of the site of the Battle of Hastings and Fortnum & Mason.

And everywhere, as I spent time in the UAE, Bahrain and later Oman, Saudi Arabia and Kuwait, I saw some of the world's worst excesses of Western consumerism . . . .

No Arab could deny this new God in the firmament. The paranoia of the new rich became an epidemic in the Middle East. Also, there was, and still is, a passion for secrecy, the need to manipulate information and the historic burdens of prejudice and self-deception. Walking in the footsteps of Good King Ready Cash were his pages, Greed and Waste!

His Excellency Sheikh Noman is a member of the royal family of Sharjah. Noman affects Western dress and had a European wife (they are separated now) and a brace of adorable children. When I knew him he had built up a thriving business empire. He had offices in West Germany and Singapore. A slim man with a hint of curly hair and a dapper moustache, Noman dismissed the fact that he was a member of the royal family of Sharjah. 'Someone has to rule, someone has to make money,' he said, offering me a Benson & Hedges. 'I make money.'

We discussed money. 'Where does it all go?' I asked.

He smiled. 'To America. We like to buy up chunks of America even if some of us get stung with hurricane belt real estate. But seriously, most of the big money goes to American banks—Citibank, Chase Manhattan, Chemical Bank. Let me put it another way: Arabs like to save their money in New York and spend it in London.'

I nodded. 'Didn't someone once say that London was the twenty-first Arab nation?'

Sheikh Noman laughed. 'Marvellous, isn't it? When it comes to having a fling the Arab really lets go. I've summered in England for many years and I am sometimes taken aback by the excesses of our people. What is more they wear their dishdashas with a swagger as though to say, "Here I am; I'm an Arab; I've got money and that makes me someone to be cultivated, robbed, titillated, conned or ambushed, whatever your present inclination is."

'I knew a stupid man from Saudi Arabia. He came to London and bought six hundred pounds worth of five penny bricks for building his house in Jeddah. Do you know what he did next? He chartered a Boeing for 27,000 pounds to take the bricks home.'

'You must be kidding.'

'Kidding? Hah! You want to see how we pander to this new sense of being rich? Go to Soho. You'll find more Arabs there than in the UAE. British women there will even kiss their arses!' He rummaged at his desk and produced an Arab newspaper. 'This is from Kuwait. The

*Al Watan*. Let me read you the editorial. It's so absurd that it's positively frightening. It says: "The Kuwaiti government should protect our citizens from exhausting themselves sexually and financially in London. It is the responsibility of the Kuwaiti government to steer our people towards proper places in London and warn them away from immoral places that rob them of their money and sexual strength." What do you think of that?'

'That,' I said, 'is disgusting.'

Soberly, he said, 'I used to think so too. Then I realized how pathetic it all is. Money is our God now. It twists our tails and drives us harder and faster than any other god. We are now kidding ourselves that we are the fabulously rich and are therefore the accepted people of the earth. What we don't see or choose not to see is the jealousy and resentment. The British are the worst and the British press reflects this jealousy and hatred of the Arab at all times. Our rulers think everything in the garden is lovely. There's one thing they don't realize—that moneybags cannot quell the world-wide and chiefly Western resentment and envy of the Arab. We may have money and we may be able to hold a lot of nations to ransom because of our oil, but we will always be to them the damn niggers who came out of the woodpile and who will never be civilized even if the UN sets up a special agency for that purpose!'

I could understand Noman's bitterness. Too much money, too suddenly, had caused a disorientation of phenomenal proportions.

'But surely,' I said, 'Islam is a great levelling force. Whatever present feelings may be, doesn't the world accept the Arab as a singularly religious person?'

Noman's eyes twinkled. 'Why do you say that?'

'Well, it's all around us, isn't it? Even as an expatriate

I cannot help but feel impressed by this positive social accent on religion. Even if the Pope had a Vatican TV programme, I doubt if this programme would be interrupted for the saying of the *Angelus*.'

'Ah, you're making a common mistake, my friend. You're looking at the wood, not at the trees.'

'You mean –'

'I mean that it pleases our sense of vanity to uphold our religion as loudly and vociferously as possible. We are not content to shout our prayers from towers and turrets. Now we are broadcasting them on radio and TV. We are taking TV cameras into our mosques and putting our Imams on the screen to read and declaim the Koran. Our mosque building is fantastic. By the end of 1985 [I interviewed him in 1984] there will be a mosque for every forty people in this country. Oh, money can do everything. Now even God cannot escape. We Arabs have become PROs—a massive publicity department for Allah!'

After tea he said: 'Of course, you cannot write any of this here.'

'I know,' I said sadly, 'but I'll keep my notes anyway.'

Yes, money counts for everything. To be without money in the Middle East is to be of a status lower than a jackal. Money must be made by hook or by crook. Richard Crompton was, at the time, Sales Manager of a rent-a-car system in Dubai. He put it in a nutshell. 'If an old-fashioned moralist were to come to Dubai, he would find more crooks here than in any other place on earth, with the possible exception of Wormwood Scrubs!'

People would tell me: 'Money is being made over and under the table and there are very high-placed people here who are swinging the deals.' And, 'Oh, there is corruption, but it depends on how you look at it. We may feel peculiar about it, but not the Arabs. Their standards are different.

They cannot and will not understand Western standards of corruption. The commission business here has become a monster—up to twenty-five per cent and more.'

All over the Middle East big international firms shell out vast sums in commission. Frances Biglegs was Sales Manager of the Consumer Division of a Dubai firm. 'Commission?' she said. 'Do you know what I must do? Raise horrified hands and ask you to please leave this office. Commission! The very idea!'

'I like your legs,' I said.

'Flatterer,' she laughed, stretching her legs out under her desk so that I could view them better. 'You don't expect me to say that we pay out commissions, do you? Even if we do, which is quite proper, we are unaware of its eventual destination.'

'And suppose you do?'

'It's a difficult situation, actually. Our firm doesn't like doing it. No British firm does. But if we don't, the Japs or Americans will. What most British firms do is show the commission as an expense and part of the contract. Usually the commission is added to the contract and becomes part of the estimate. It's unethical, of course, but it does give us more foreign exchange because we pay out in dirhams anyway . . .'

Yes, in the Middle East religion is not an opium for the masses. Rather, it is a cold compress that is laid on the forehead to ease the hot flush of feverish money-making.

People in Dubai lead a humdrum life. The workers, that is. Thus, they like to gossip. A newsman on his rounds hears things. When it comes to Arab extravagance the stories are too many to record here. Some choice tidbits come to mind, however. Like the two Saudi princes who ran short of spending money in New York and got the

Bank of America to send them an after hours delivery of US$200,000 for the weekend.

'There was this Arab who went to London . . . ' is the familiar beginning to many of these believe-it-or-nots. One is expected to brace oneself to listen to something that is guaranteed to curl the hair on one's chest.

' . . . and he paid 350 pounds for a pound of strawberries!'

' . . . and he bought six 10,000-pound mink coats. He said they made excellent bathrobes!'

' . . . and he went to a dentist. The bill was £ 50.00 but he didn't see the decimal. He wrote a cheque for £ 5000. The dentist told him it was only fifty pounds and you know what he did? Told the dentist to cash the cheque because he wasn't going to bother writing another cheque!'

Desmond Dylan, Marketing Manager of an international cargo system did a lot of business in Dubai. His Dubai agents were a cargo agency of long standing. On one of his visits from England he told me: 'You should see the Arabs, especially Arab women, who flock to Marks & Spencer. In the Marble Arch outlet, sales to Arabs are about one million pounds a week. Arab women buy racks of dresses and knickers by the thousands. Then they squat on the pavement with their purchases and unpick the St Michael labels so that no one home will know that they have been to a Jewish shop.'

One story out of Marks & Spencer holds special appeal. The store had brought in 12,000 dozens of men's underpants from Paris. Each had an ornate label which was thought to be a neat piece of abstract art. Along came a Saudi businessman who promptly bought the lot. The label on each pair of underpants was a copy of a thirteenth century Arabic script which read: There is no God but Allah.

## A Funny Thing Happened

Lots of things can happen when modern Western materialism seduces Middle Eastern philosophy. To survive, one has to keep one's cool. Naturally, the stark realities of business contradict the official platitudes which are mouthed for public consumption. As a newsman I had it up to here with the platitudes!

God and Mammon, I fear, are headed for a clash in the Gulf.

I also know that God, being a peaceable bloke and having no use for money, will cop out!

# Rub-A-Dub-Dub

Spit and polish! Oh, the pride, the joy,
It's all you do to be a Navy boy,
Ay, there's the rub—that wretched bottom line
When quartermasters bid you Rise and Shine!

In the 1950s the Commanding Officer of the Royal Ceylon Naval Training Camp, HMCyS Rangalla, was Lieutenant Dharrumph, who maintained, pleasantly enough, that sailors are made, not born.

'You're here to be trained,' he said in his almost musical voice, 'and this is something we are good at. Very good at. There will be parade every morning and you will learn to love your boots and your brass and look after them. You may swear at everything—the master-at-arms, the watch bell, the guards instructor, even at me, the cooks, the staff . . .' he beamed, 'that's all right. Everybody must swear. Gets rid of the bad feelings. And then I will punish you until you fall in a fucking heap and never open your dirty mouths again! *You got that?*'

I stared. I had never seen someone so affable one minute and so venomous the next. No, Lieutenant Dharrumph's smile was a storm warning of sorts.

Led to our messes, each of us claimed bunk and locker. 'Get your bloody fingers out!' an Able Seaman snarled. 'Collect your sheets, blankets, get shipshape!'

Simmons told Aloysius: 'Once more you say you want to go home, I'll brain you!'

The recriminations came. 'All this damn polishing polishing, what the hell is this? Just look at that parade ground. Red dust! You polish and polish and in two seconds your boots are covered in dust!'

I had a point, of course, but there was no help to it. Boots had to be disguised as mirrors. Caps had to be Meltonian cleaned to look like Snow White's knickers. Ordinary Seaman Van Langenburg gave a superior sniff. 'I don't mind,' he said grandly. 'My uncle is in the Army and he showed me how to polish boots. See . . . first take a little polish on your finger and rub it well into the leather. Then spit and rub that well in. The polish gets nice and smooth . . . .'

We watched interestedly and put our heads together.

'So, Van Langenburg, you like this polishing business?'

'Oh yes. Even at home, I polish the shoes for everybody. How do you like this toecap now? Like silk.'

Boots sailed in from all corners. Van Langenburg leaped off his bunk.

'You say you like it,' I sang out, 'so you polish.'

'What? You're mad? How can I polish all this?'

'Hmmmm . . . let's see. Thirty pairs only.'

'You're mad? I'll be polishing all evening. Thirty pairs! You fellows are joking, right?'

'Just take them one by one. That's the best way.'

'Oh no! Polish your own boots!'

'Oh all right. You can't rely on anyone these days. But don't sleep at night, OK?'

'Wha-what? Why can't I sleep at night?'

'Oh by all means sleep. But we're thinking, it might be better if you don't.'

'Hah! You're trying to do something to me while I'm sleeping? Just you try it! I'll make a complaint! This is a hell of a thing . . . I must polish everybody's boots?'

'OK, OK, so don't. We'll polish our own boots. We know what to do.'

'What?'

'That doesn't concern you.'

Van Langenburg became quite nervous. 'But-but this is not fair. Not fair at all!'

'Fair? You're the one who boasted that you like polishing. Polish for your family. So what's the problem now? And anyway, we said no, don't bother. So what's wrong now?'

'But you said not to sleep.'

'Yes.'

'Why?'

'Why not? If we are up, why must you sleep?'

Van Langeburg's head swam. 'You're mad. Just see. I have to work on these boots for about fifteen minutes.'

'Yes, we can see. But you take fifteen minutes and look at your boots. Like straight from the shop. Just look at ours. I've been rubbing these effing things for about an hour. Look at this. Just look. It looks as if it has been up and down a monkey's arse! Can't you understand that you're the best guy for the job?'

'But how? Thirty pairs!' Van Langenburg wailed. 'I can't!'

'Why can't you? We are all in the same hut. If you can't cooperate go to another hut. Go and tell that Leading Seaman fellow. I saw how he was looking at you. Might take you to his bunk in the night.'

Van Langenburg looked bleakly at the pile of boots, then took one up. 'What about all the other work?'

'What work?'

'Why, the webbing and brass and all.'

'You give those here. We will do that. You just sit and

polish. You want tea, we'll bring you your tea also.' So Van Langenburg polished and was thanked prettily for his pains and Hut Three marched with a twinkle in their toes until everything went to pieces at Colour Guard one morning.

I must explain that each morning, the white naval ensign is hoisted and a band of recruits make up the Colour Guard. Colours are hoisted at eight a.m. and struck at sunset. The Guard has to salute the ensign which a Signalman slowly hoists, then secures. At sunset, usually six p.m. or nautically, 1800 hours, the colours are brought down. This is a daily ritual.

'God help us all!' screamed the Platoon Commander. 'Ordinary Seaman Van Langenburg! Fall out!'

This manoeuvre executed, the PC called the Duty Officer to witness. 'Sir, look at his fingers, sir!'

Everybody looked. On a hillock overlooking the parade ground where another mast and yardarm were in business, the Preparatory pennant fluttered up on the halyard.

'Five minutes to Colours, sir,' a Leading Seaman carolled.

'Fall in!' the Duty Officer roared. 'After colours you'll see stars, my lad!'

Having duly presented arms, Van Langenburg was hauled out of rank again. The Platoon Commander gave him a withering look. 'Tell me . . . tell me how you come on Parade with some black shit all over your fingers . . . stand erect! Don't fidget like you got bloody threadworms! Well?'

'Sir, I was polishing boots, sir.'

'Look, you bloody clown, one pair of boots to polish for morning divisions and you get polish up to your fucking elbows? Look at your fingernails!' and rolling his eyes heavenwards, 'Is this a bloody seaman or a fucking lunatic?'

Nobody up there offered an opinion.

'All the boots,' Van Langenburg muttered.

'All the boots? What boots? Are you mad? *Are you trying to drive me mad?*'

The dam burst. 'Thirty pairs! Thirty bloody pairs every day! This is why I joined the Navy? To polish these other buggers' boots?' He thrust a hand under the PC's nose. 'See my fucking hands. And I must stand here and listen to you? What the fuck do you know? I'm a bloody clown . . . I'm a bloody lunatic . . . it's damn easy for you to stand there and say whatever comes into your fucking head! You with your white shoes. Huh! You don't have to polish them!'

The Colour Guard was in convulsions. The Duty Officer stepped discreetly away. The Platoon Commander blanched. This is a recruit. A recruit! 'Fall in!' he screamed. 'Stand erect! Stand still the rest of you! Ordinary Seaman Van Langenburg report to the Regulating Office at ten hundred hours!'

Van Langenburg didn't budge. He regarded the PC sourly. 'Rubbish!' he said. 'All bloody rubbish! Ten hundred hours! Why can't you say ten o'clock like normal people? Huh! Bloody mad buggers you all are!' and he swaggered back, rifle tilted crazily on his shoulder.

'Colour Guard will retire! Aaaa-baht tarn! Deeees-miss!'

'Like hell,' Van Langenburg snarled and, carrying his rifle like a scythe, strode to the Regulating Office where a fat-faced Malay quartermaster raised an eyebrow.

'Whadd'you'want?'

Freezing the man with a look, Van Langenburg shouldered past.

No one knew what transpired in that Regulating Office. Sick Bay Attendant Winnie told Ordinary Signalman 'Daft' Fernando, 'Shame, men. Don't know what will happen to him. Shouldn't have made him polish our boots.'

The others hung around, waiting, wondering.

'Pssst! He's coming,' Ordinary Telegraphist Carlo Nugara hissed.

Van Langenburg emerged. He carried his rifle as carelessly as ever and Simmons remarked that his bayonet had been stripped. True, there was no fixed bayonet. It hung demurely within the 'frog' on the web belt. We creased foreheads, trying to interpret this sign. Van Langenburg came up, fixed wrathful eyes on us, strode into the hut and flung his rifle with a thump on the bunk. Then he spun round and seized Ordinary Telegraphist Thiagalingam by the throat. 'Gum,' he grated, 'gimme some gum.'

Thiagalingam's eyes bulged. He was a small-made cheery little Tamil who grinned a lot and had very white teeth in a very black face. 'Here! Let go!' he burbled. He was growing purple, which, on black, made him look awful.

'Gum,' Van Langenburg growled, taking his hand away and leaving a blacker smear on a black neck. Thiagalingam knew that it was not his to reason why. If gum was the need of the moment, gum he would provide. In pots. In barrels if desired. He opened his locker with nerveless fingers.

'Hey, George,' Todd sang out, 'what happ—'

'You shut up!' Van Langenburg snatched at the tube of Gripfix and extracted a sheet of paper from his hip pocket. Smearing it with glue, he swung the door shut and slapped on the paper. Then he turned and grinned. 'If you can't shine your boots you can go and shit in them!' he said grandly.

It was an order from the C. O.

ALL RATINGS WILL POLISH THEIR OWN BOOTS OR ELSE

'Or else what?' Electricians Mate Koelmeyer demanded.

'That you go and ask,' Van Langenburg was relaxing on his bunk. 'Go and ask if you like.'

Nobody wished to, but matters did not end there, for Carlo Nugara had a brainwave when mucking around in the paint store one morning. He gave his work boots a gentle coating of Black Japan and lo! they shone with a faery light. With little croaks of delight he rushed to the hut and stood before us in twin pools of glory. We gaped.

'What the hell did you do?' asked someone with a catch in his voice.

'Painted the bloody things! Now how? No more polishing. Just wipe. And if they get scratched or anything, just put on more paint.' He gave Van Langenburg a pitying look. 'You rub,' he said condescendingly, 'one brush of paint and our work's over.'

Even Van Langenburg took notice. 'My God, that sort of shine who can get? Like enamel, no? So what are we sitting here and rubbing and brushing? Let's paint the fucking things!'

In a mass we descended on the paint stores and the Platoon Commander was in ecstasies on the following morning. Being at best, quite a sarcastic prune, he even permitted a little smile to twitch the corner of his lip. He said, huskily, that he wished to congratulate us on our most seamanlike turnout. He even hinted that he would have to wear sunglasses the next day and revelled in each pair of boots in much the same way as one would if one, while sitting in a bistro in Rome, suddenly found Sophia Loren in one's lap. We ha-ha'd politely. We knew he was trying to be jovial and pitied him immensely. His order to dismiss was almost sugary. As we marched away, the sun drawing lines of silver on the Black Japan, we heard him give a small squeal of satisfaction.

It took a few days for the paint to crack. Who the devil thought it would? It flaked off in bits and pieces and cobwebbed in hideous wrinkles and scrawls. Ordinary Telegraphist Yusuf threw up his arms and announced that he wished most earnestly to kill himself.

'Never mind that. You can kill yourself afterwards. What are we going to do now?'

Aloysius groaned. 'Will have to dump them in kerosene oil or something and scrape the paint off.'

We went into a huddle. Each had two pairs of boots, true, but one pair was used for everyday work parties, fatigues and general clumping around camp. Parades, divisions, colour guards and all other ceremonial hoo-ha required the other pair. We cast hopeful eyes on our work boots but the general opinion was that these looked as though they had been laid in line and sodomized by a hippopotamus. But, at least, they weren't encrusted in paint. They could be brought to scratch.

We formed rank for Colour Guard the next morning with the distinct feeling that all would not be well.

'Muller! Your boots are a bloody disgrace!'

I scorned reply. It was no good telling this excitable man that I had laboured, yes laboured, from eight o'clock to lights out, grimly bringing my work boots to a semblance of the ceremonial. True, they were not beautiful, but quite winsome, I thought. A sort of homely beauty. I had felt as though I was performing some sort of archaeological restoration.

'Answer me! Why are your boots not polished?'

I looked straight ahead. 'I polished them, sir.'

'Hah! What did you do? Rubbed them on your bum?'

'No, sir.'

'What was that?'

'No, sir. I didn't think of that, sir. Next time I will, sir.'

'What the fuck are you talking about? Fall out! *Fall out!* FALL OUT!'

I fell out. Very excitable, this character.

The old song of the Leading Seaman sounded across the parade ground. 'Five minutes to Colours, sir.'

Meanwhile, the rest of the squad, also asked to fall out, were each standing wherever they had fallen out and the Platoon Commander was ready for a cosy session with a psychiatrist. The signalman on the hill began jiggling the Preparatory pennant. One minute to eight o'clock. The PC shut his eyes in anguish, then opened them and screamed: 'What are you all doing out of rank? *Fall in!* FALL IN! Squad . . . . hough! Slope . . . arrmmhz!'

Fantastic. As the white ensign climbed gracefully we presented arms in general salute. The screech of the bosun's pipe died away. It was time for Act One, Scene Two.

'Will you bastards kindly tell me why you conspire to *drive me crazy at eight o'clock in the fucking morning!*'

No answer.

'You! YES YOU!' a quivering finger stabs in the direction of Cook Steward Haramanis. 'Why are your boots not polished this morning?'

Haramanis, who is most uncomfortable with the English language and who only joined the Navy to sit in a galley and cook, says, 'Eh?'

Eyes roll, seeking divine aid. 'I suppose all of you polished your boots for morning colours?' Quite reasonable, the tone of voice.

'Yes, sir.'

'I see . . .' still the sweet tone of reason. 'Yes, Todd, you did polish your little booties, didn't you? You sat on your little bunk with a little boot in your hand and you polished and polished, didn't you?'

Todd looked down hastily. He has size nine feet and wears size ten boots. Call that little? 'Yes, sir.'

'How long did you take to polish your boots, Todd?'

'Almost an hour, sir.'

'LIAR !' He was off again. 'What do you take me for? WHAT DO YOU TAKE ME FOR? One hour you polished to come on parade like this?'

Todd believed that it took two to tango. He remained silent.

'You know what I think? None of you polished your boots last night. ISN'T THAT SO?'

No answer.

'All right! I'll show you buggers. This is mutiny, do you hear? MUTINY! You all thought you could come on parade with dirty boots. That's it. That's it! Right . . . HIGH PORT ARMS!'

Mechanically rifles were raised over heads, held up at arm's length.

'Squad will advance! Lef' Tarrrn! At the double . . . marrrch!'

And there we were, the entire Colour Guard, running all over the parade ground, rifles aloft, round and round, this way, that way, any way, with the Platoon Commander hooting 'PICK YOUR FEET UP THERE! Hup hup hup hup . . . Abarrrt tarrrn! HUP HUP HUP HUP HUP!' It was hard to tell what was more ridiculous—the squad bouncing around with rifles held up like trophies of war, or the PC who trotted behind screaming 'hup hup hup'.

'Do these buggers get as mad as this so early in the morning?' I gasped and Ordinary Seaman Jayasinghe puffed and huffed and gritted that his arms were numb.

The sad case of the boots was finally solved with the liberal application of turpentine and a great deal of cajoling to make the ill-treated leather respond. Simmons was the least patient. 'Is this why we joined this fucking Navy?' he demanded. He had a corn, and the unscheduled morning sprint had not done it much good. 'To polish and pipeclay and arrange bunks! Huh!' He scowled mightily and spat a blob on his toecap.

Todd rose, stretched wearily. 'Hup hup hup hup,' he sang and we dissolved into helpless laughter.

# Ups And Downs

> See, saw, up and down,
> English has got its new masters,
> Spread the good word for many a day
> Till every young mind's a disaster!

As Johnson once said, one needs to peregrinate in the metropolis . . . which beats walking about any day.

In my home town, Kandy, Sunday evenings are pretty quiet. People like to stay home and brood about the Monday morning peregrination to work. But, in many nooks and crannies, young people gather in eager-beaver groups to sit before their several gurus who 'with words of learned length and thund'ring sound' conduct their Squeers schools of English.

So lucrative has this business become that several Philistines who are confident that 'photon' is the plural of 'photo' and a 'hippodrome' is the place in the local zoo where the hippo resides, have set up large tutories to inflict on aspiring, perspiring young people, the art and craft of the spoken word.

All over Kandy, the Queen's English is being clubbed, bludgeoned, shot, stabbed, axed to death after an incredible period of brutal torture and mutilation. Being born inquisitive, I joined a boy of my locality. He was setting out to his weekly class. Now I've known this lad, Sarath, for a couple of years. He is a likeable fellow, and like thousands of other likeable fellows in this country, is unemployed. He began this Spoken English gig a couple of months ago but refuses to speak with me in English. Oh, he does seek clarification once in a way. Like the day he asked: 'Uncle, what is foliage?' (This 'uncle' business is very common in these parts. Young bucks give respect by calling a man 'uncle').

He is not satisfied when I tell him that this means the leaves of plants collectively. He insists that I explain in Sinhala. I gave up on him on the day he saw me burning a pile of dry leaves in my garden. 'Ah,' he nodded wisely, 'foliage burning, no?'

But I decided to check out Sarath's class. I came back, walking on egg shells. Dream-like awe. A sublime awareness that here, around me, were several mills grinding away, making with assiduous zeal a whole generation of monkey-on-a-stick youngsters who would go into the world, open their mouths and become the laughing stock of the ages!

The 'master' was impressive. Cut-away coat, badly knotted tie, owlish spectacles and a dome devoid of hair. Something between Telly Savalas and Benito Mussolini. He stood at a table. Before him serried ranks of benches and long tables now filling up with his eighty bucks per month pupils who called him 'master' and 'sir' and acclaimed, 200-strong, that he was their destiny.

At 16,000 bucks per month, tax free, he was pleased to be their destiny. Who wouldn't?

He taught through a microphone.

'This is organized class,' said Sarath enthusiastically.

I lolled near the barn door. Bloody marvellous, I thought. Here were red-blooded boys who thought nothing of slinging mud balls at policemen and hooting their schoolmasters hoarse. Now, keen on the murder of the English language, they troop in, sit, ogle the girls who giggle back and await that final tap on the mike which signals the beginning of the class.

'Today we will look at this sentence.'

On a mildewed blackboard appears the startling news: *I went to Colombo by the down train.*

Class is puzzled. What is down train?

'*Aday!* You don't know simple thing like that? What for I'm teaching and teaching I don't know. Kandy is up, no? We are uda (up) in the hills no? What is uda?'

'Up!' comes the chorus.

'So when you go to Colombo going down, no?'

Vigorous nods.

'So train going down is down train, right?'

Light in every eye.

The word 'down' is underlined with a flourish.

'Now we will study this. Down. Train is going down. You know that now—'

'Down the hill,' a bright voice says.

Master beams. 'Very good. Hill going down to Colombo. Now what is meaning of down?'

'Hill,' many suggest half-heartedly.

'Yes, yes, but what is to go? All right, what is to sit down?'

'On the backside to wait.'

'Good. So you sit down. On bench, no?'

Everybody nods. One raises a hand. 'Pliss sir, how to spell banch?'

'Banch not, men, bench! B-e-n-c-h.'

Pens fly over notebooks. 'Down' is 'bench'.

'Then lie down is what?' somebody asks.

'Why you buffalo, where you lie down?'

'On bed.'

'So what is so hard to understand? Why I am teaching and teaching like this? Sit down on bench, on chair, on

157

ground, on step. Lie down on mat, on bed, on settee if you like. On ground also. All this is down. Now say loud, I sit down.'

'*I sit down.*'

'I lie down.'

'*I lie down.*'

'I go down.'

'*I go down*—pliss sir, how you go down? By the train?'

'By the legs, men! If I say I go down the well you can go in the well in the train? This is hell of a buffalo!' he tells the rest of the class.

Loud cackles. 'Oi, Nimal,' someone calls, 'you get inside the well in a train?'

'So now,' master rubs his hands, 'down is to get down. It is opposite of up.'

Hands shoot roofwards.

'Yes, yes, I know,' the master says, 'that is big word, no? Opposite is not. So down is not up and up is not down.'

That takes some thinking. I see painful furrows appear.

At last the glimmerings take hold.

'You must know these meanings,' the master says piously, 'that girl there . . . you, Chandrika, yes, stand up. Make for me a sentence. You know? Make sentence with the opposite. Now you were hearing no? Opposite is not, you understand? Others write down—Opposite of down is up. What's the matter? Everything I must spell? Fine thing this is, no? Oppo-zeet! O-p-p-o-s-e-e-t. Right? Now write. Down is not up. Up is not down. So that is meaning of opposite. Right. Now Chandrika make sentence. Just tell.'

Chandrika is blushing. 'With opposite?' she asks.

'Yes, yes. If I say you are going home after class what is opposite?'

'But I'm going to big sister's place. Tomorrow having big almsgiving. To help I'm going.'

'What are you going on? Make, will you, sentence!'

Chandrika crimsoms. 'After class I opposite home.'

'What is that? How you can opposite home?'

'Becos I'm going sister's home.'

'So what do we care where you are going? What for you are saying you are opposite home? You must say you are NOT going home.'

Chandrika nods happily. There, that's straightened out at last.

'You must say, after class I am not going home. That is right way English. If you say opposite home is opposite house. Opposite is other side.'

Chandrika sits down. This is getting unreal. If opposite is other side, what happened to 'not'? Real sambol, this English business.

Someone stands up. 'In newspaper back page have funny word. Dressing down. What sir is this dressing down?'

'Man, what you are talking? When you put on your clothes you are dressing up, no?'

Everybody nods. One chants, 'I am dressing UP to go DOWN to Colombo.'

Master beams. 'Very good. Vaary good. Now see, I am dressing up to come and teach you.'

'Then dressing down?'

'How you can dress down? Everybody here dressing up. Only you want to dress down?'

'But in the paper—'

'What, I say, everyday in papers have mistakes, no? How you know that is correct? When printing paper making lot of mistakes. I know! Must be dressing gown.

159

Like that housecoat thing ladies wearing. That is dressing gown.'

'But this is rugger news, sir,' the voice says stubbornly. 'Bloomfield club gave Havelocks club dressing down.'

'Aha! Dressing gown must be. Anyone can give anyone else a dressing gown, no? If you are reading papers how you can learn English? Every week I coming teaching and teaching and you are going and reading papers. Fine thing this is.'

Class over, I walked back with Sarath in silence.

'So, Uncle, how our master?' he cadged a verdict.

I shot him a murderous look. I wanted to go home, dress up, take a down train and go somewhere opposite Colombo!

# With Flying Colours

> From masthead high the flag astounds the sky
> The halyards twang as proud the colours fly,
> But save our souls! it signifies distress,
> That errant yeoman's put us in a mess!

Everyone's proud of a flag. Hoist the colours and it does something to you. It gives you a sort of lift; puts your soul on an escalator. Your mind begins to swell.

In Sri Lanka we honour many flags. Colours, too, are significant, and of all the flags we raise, nothing is more striking, than the Buddhist flag with its many stripes and patches of colour.

I suppose all those colours mean something. But when this flag was jacked up on the main mast of the H.M.Cy.S *Vijaya* in 1954, the captain of H.M.C.S. Okapi, a Royal Canadian destroyer, blinked and blinked again. True, he was in the exotic east where strange things usually happen, but never had he seen such a peculiar signal.

The *Vijaya* was primed to move out of Colombo harbour, Captain Donald Victor Hunter in command. First Bloke or Number One was Lieutenant Wahid, and on board were a brave contingent of the Ceylon Army under Colonel Sepala Attygalla and an equally daring cohort of fly boys of the Ceylon Air Force. Two journalists from the local press were also on board. I stood at the guard rails, looking down on the Queen Elizabeth Quay alongside which we were moored.

November 1953. The north-east monsoon was howling its head off in the Bay of Bengal and forty-foot waves were the order of the day. It was a grey morning with a bad weather smell and a whippy wind that seemed to threaten: 'Just you come out of harbour and see what I will do!'

Stirring, fervent things were happening on the quay. There were squads of Buddhist monks. There were gung-ho military and naval types. There were citizens of many stripes. Some strutted around as much as to say: 'See how important I am', while others wore that cosmetic confidence that said, 'I am also here', and edged around to get into the frames of the press cameras.

The *Vijaya*—Sri Lanka's only minesweeper—was ready to make an epic voyage to Burma. We, the crew, had been told, and quite fiercely too, that we were henceforth ambassadors of our country. To stress this, a pugnacious little squirt of a man, Cook-Steward Jamis, was drafted on board. He went beserk somewhere between the Andamans and the Nicobars and had to be locked up in the shipwright's store.

Yeoman of Signals Ranasinghe trotted between boat deck and signals deck in shining white. He was quite taken up with the whole ceremony. He was also an ardent Buddhist and actually knew how to swear in Sanskrit.

On the quay, oil lamps were lit and the covey of monks began a sonorous chant. We stood patiently, adopting demeanours of rapt attention. We, the ship, the captain, the sea, the barnacles on our bottom were all subject to a carpet blessing. Meanwhile, a crane trundled up on parallel rails and readied itself to lift on board our most important passenger: Lord Buddha himself. Bronze, heavy, lotus positioned.

Nineteen fifty-four was special. It was the year of the Buddha Jayanti—a celebration to mark the second millennium of Buddhism in the world and in Asia in particular. It was the year to knit some good wool between neighbouring Buddhist lands. The government of Sri Lanka had to make a show of it. The Ministry of Culture and the Ministry of Foreign Affairs came up with the idea. Carry across the Indian Ocean a special gift to the Government of Burma. Let's make it big. After all, we are a small country. Also, let's show the Burmese that we have a navy.

Now that, in 1954, was a matter of debate. We had one warship. The others were seaward defence boats and a larger coastal patrol named the *Kotiya*. As a navy we were in the Hawaiian class in the time of Queen Likelike—and even she, I am told, had more war canoes.

But we had the *Vijaya*, and, with its forty-foot mast and displacement of 1,040 tons and complement of ninety-six, this tub (it was the Canadian *Flying Fish* until we took it over and gave it a lick of paint) was the best we had.

For the cruise, the *Vijaya* was grossly overcrowded. The tiny wardroom with its additional Army and Air Force officers was ready to burst and the mess system was shaken out and stood on its ear. The seamen's mess was turned over to the Air Force and the communication's mess to the Army. This latter was a grave mistake. The mess was for'rad, slap against the bows and any sailor will tell you that that's the worst place to be in if you are a landlubber. It's the bows that take the pitch and toss. The Army groaned and vomited and wept and those who could talk declared that they were dead. That was on the first day out . . . and we hadn't hit the rough weather.

The seamen's mess had its own comforts. It took in water. There was no particular reason for this, but Able Seaman Mendis rose one morning to see his boots float by and blistered the bulkhead with his oaths.

The Air Force men, consigned to bed down here, were convinced that they would never see Burma. It was all well and good for the Indian Ocean to remain beyond the steel, but it wasn't welcome in their sleeping quarters.

So, in addition to its ninety-six men and four officers, there were twenty-four 'other services' and their four officers as well as a brace of journalists. We had to spread canvas on the boat deck. Wet weather put paid to that and there was a rush for the galley tables. Jamis couldn't take the pressure. He wrenched off a brass tap from its socket and split open an able seaman's head.

But all that could be considered part of the drama of the voyage. The first shots were fired, seemingly, by our devout Yeoman of Signals. He had, unknown to the captain and crew, brought a Buddhist flag on board, tucked it into the flag locker and breathlessly bided his time.

Amid rising chants of praise from the pier, the huge bronze of the Buddha was swung aboard. Over the guard rails, between the lifeboat stanchions. Captain Hunter supervized the soft, precise landing. The statue was steadied, then carefully lowered inch by inch to the deck, slap against the vegetable locker which was the only large structure in sight. On either side of this locker were the gangways to the quarter-deck where tracks led to the depth charge barrels and the paravanes for minesweeping and retrieval. Here also was the after-steering compartment with its big ship's wheel.

The statue looked secure enough. Able Seaman

Jackson creased his brow. 'So where do we show the films?' he asked.

A Chief Petty Officer sniffed. 'No films on this trip,' he said.

'Why?'

'Why? Can't you see that the locker can't be used?'

Painfully true. We used to sling the canvas screen on the locker. Now the statue was in the way.

'So no films?'

'How many times have I got to tell you, you idiot!'

Exit Jackson, swearing foully.

No sooner did the statue touch down than the harbour sucked back in wonderment. From the flag deck, rising on the main mast halyard, tautening on its butterfly clips, was a strange flag. A flag that no naval or international signal book had any answer for. Yeoman Ranasinghe was well pleased. He had honoured the statue of Lord Buddha. The Buddhist flag slapped proudly in the morning wind.

From its berth, the Canadian destroyed *Okapi* (which was on a routine visit to Colombo) sprang into action. A ten-inch visual lantern was turned on us and flashed its concern. 'What is the trouble? We are ready to slip moorings and come alongside to render assistance.'

Hunter tore at the forelock he liked to twirl around his finger. Ranasinghe blanched as the skipper's roar knifed through the air. Without waiting for more, he ducked out of sight, then, bent in two, he crept down the gangway.

'Muller! What the fuck is that?'

'Sir, what, sir?'

'That, you fool! What's that flag up there? Who hoisted that? Get it down at once! Is this a fucking warship or what? Who hoisted that? Who? I want to know who!

And—here! come here! I haven't finished! Where the fuck are you going?'

'To take the flag down sir.'

'Signal the *Okapi* and say no trouble.'

'Yes, sir.'

'Pull that flag down!'

'Yes, sir.'

'So go!'

I went. Of Ranasinghe there was no sign. Mind, he didn't get into any real hot water. It was dismissed as a serious bout of Buddhistic fervour. Despite my assuring signal, the *Okapi* had put out a whaler and a Canadian lieutenant and a leading seaman came aboard, quite anxious and seeking assurance that all was well. They were also most interested.

'So what is that flag?' the leading seaman asked.

We explained.

'Never saw one like that before.'

Few naval vessels in the world have. Navy signals are mysterious. Anything that cannot be read, identified or interpreted is looked on as a distress signal. This includes any flag that has been hoisted upside down, or the raising of a bucket and a blanket or, as in this case, a totally unidentifiable flag. No wonder it raised such concern.

Ranasinghe was unrepentant. He said it was his Buddhist duty to signal the importance of our mission. 'This is a religious cruise,' he said. 'We are taking a statue of the Buddha as a gift to Burma.'

'But this is the navy,' I said.

'You wait and see,' he said darkly. 'We will have trouble on this trip.'

A cracked skull and a mad cook were only part of it. It took us ten days to make the crossing in the worst weather imaginable and even after being piloted up the Rangoon river our troubles did not end.

But that's another story.

# Guide Me, I'm A Tourist

This land of rare delights and vistas new,
Such sights to see, and lots of things to do;
Come, look upon me as your leading light,
Your guiding star, your friend, your local blight!

At sporadic intervals the Tourist Board of Sri Lanka and that snifty bunch who revel in the name of the Tourist Police put heads together and decide that enough is enough.

They deplore the fact that many strange people who claim to be tourist guides of sorts, gather in droves to bemuse, bewilder, bother and befuddle visitors with their spiel, and demonstrate with verve and vigour the glories of the island as seen through the eyes of sundry jackasses.

It may be all well and good to haul a discomfited Norwegian to the 'botnik' gardens and tell him in thrilling tones that 'Bambu' is the local word for 'Bamboo', but when these local shepherds lead their flock on what is a carefully mapped-out 'commission scramble', things begin to get quite unpleasant.

Tourists to Sri Lanka suddenly find that they have this wily latcher-on who is hell-bent on leading them like a latter-day Moses to a promised land of sleazy shops and questionable emporiums. They are taken to a central market where they are encouraged to pat pineapples and lovingly stroke long yellow bananas, and thereon arm-wrestled into dubious shops where they are offered the most incredible junk in Asia.

Such shenanigans made the authorities most annoyed. In Kandy, the capital of the hill country, over fifty of these so-called guides were recently coralled, hauled up before the Beak and fined. The constabulary and the tourist cops were charged to take a very dim view of the activities of these 'guides' and discourage (with a few swift kicks wherever possible) all such parasitical perambulations.

The city became too hot for them. But there's this thing about any leech. It won't say die. They began to apply their talents elsewhere and, to the annoyance (and amusement) of many, began to operate in the intercity express train which plies daily between Colombo and Kandy.

This is an interesting mode of conveyance and well-patronized by foreigners. It is a three-hour, non-stop run in either direction. There is canned music and reserved seats and toilets that have just started to smell. The train runs express past stations and stops at signals, which, all agree, is the tradition for express trains all over the world.

I have reason to travel from my hometown in Kandy to Colombo. The Intercity is a tolerably swift way to get there and back. This, then, is a ball-by-ball commentary of one such trip . . .

It is most disconcerting at times to even consider that one could be mistaken for a tourist. One expects these guides to know, at least, who is a tourist and who isn't. Apparently they don't. Play the field, seems to be the motto. Accost any fair skin in sight.

So here comes this spivvy character. He wears a pair

174

of Italian shoes two sizes larger than his feet. He stops, gives a wheedly smile and says, 'Guten morgen, you are Germany, no?'

I agree. I am Germany no. I am Sri Lanka yes.

He flashes sixteen teeth. The others seem to have missed the train. Also, I am reading, and this fellow with his bow legs and his big shoes insists on yipping into my ear like a Pomeranian that has taken to Politics.

Eventually, I tell him in patient Sinhala that I am no German and the closest I have ever got to anything Teutonic was the bout of German measles I had when I was a child. (There *was* this German girl once, but that won't bear mention!)

This stopped him dead. His jaw dropped—not a pretty sight with all those truant molars—and he backed away, confused. So he had dropped a clanger. Never mind. There must be other fish to fry.

Our train had taken in its fair share of tourists in Kandy and I was interested to know how Bow Legs fared. Drifting to the restaurant car I found him chatting up a tourist couple. The male had a high-domed head, very shiny spectacles and ears like tubas. The female was a homely, frizzy-haired lady with very pale blue eyes. She was clad in something that looked like the pyjamas of a boarder in Trinity College. Both were considering the eggburgers on their plates with concern.

I must mention that the restaurant car is very proud of these things. They take a bun, slice it open, stick in a salad leaf, some tomato shavings and a wedge of omelette. The result sans salt, mayonnaise or any sort of flavour, is an eggburger. It has this distinct taste of bread and brown paper.

Our man, wise in the ways of his breed, had settled for a three-cornered bread roll which had been stuffed with a crackling hot 'sambol'—a relish of fried onion and chilli powder. He is in his element. He has found his quarry, latched on, and actually provided them with eggburgers. Now, he believes, they are everlastingly in his debt.

Politeness forces the tourists to roll their eyes heavenwards and nibble. Our man is at his brightest. He indicates his half-eaten roll. 'This is hot. That is why I not get like this for you. This have hot hot chilli.'

The couple nod gamely.

'This is hot dog. You like hot dog?'

The couple are examining their shreds of tomato clinically.

'This dog have sambol. Very hot.'

Tuba Ears pricks up. 'Dog?' he says.

'What I eating. Sambol dog.'

Frizzy Hair tosses most of her eggburger out of the window.

Snack time over, conversation gets on a better footing. Yes, they are going to Colombo. That's what their tickets say. Do trains in Sri Lanka tend to change their minds half way? They are to stay in a guest house in Havelock Town.

Bow Legs tells them that they must not take any taxi. Why, he knows all the taxis in Colombo. He will take them safely to their guest house. Have they been to the zoo? How about the museum? And what about the Kelaniya temple? Has Tuba Ears got a spare shirt? 'I from Kandy, but if you like I can stay one two days in Colombo to help you. You just say what you like to do.'

He expands wonderfully. 'All tourists my friends. I have aunty in Colombo. We can go and visit. You like that I think. Have back room in guest house for guides, no? You have changed dollars? Where? Tch, tch, why you go to the bank? Tchach! If you met me in Kandy I can get for you very good rate. So never mind, but I have good places in Colombo also. You tell when you want to change . . .

'See, we are now in Polgahawela. This is coconut tree place. Only two bags you have? That is nice camera. I had camera also but my son broke. Must be cheap in your country, no? You give a little, I'll take your picture. I will hold it when we come to Colombo. Full of rogue people in Colombo. Every time you must watch your things . . .

'Even taxi fellows big rogues. You don't worry. I look after everything. See, that is water bird in paddy field. White birds are kokas. Having lot of kokas in paddy fields.'

'Kokas?' says Tuba Ears weakly.

'Cranes, I think,' Frizzy Hair murmurs.

'These trees all rubber. Have rubber growing here everywhere. You went to tea factory? Tchach! If I met in Kandy can take to see. All Tamil women in tea estates. That is why Tamil mans are angry in the North. No women they are saying and fighting. How many people have in your country? Here having too much. Everywhere people. You have childrens? No? I poor man. Having fourteen childrens now. How to feed? But you kind persons I can tell.'

Colombo. Bow Legs, this modern-day succubus, jauntily leads his charges to the barrier. He ushers them into a red three-wheeler with the words LUCKY BABY painted on its derrière. They shudder away.

Shrugging, I went about my day's business and returned to the railway station for the return express to Kandy. And there was Bow Legs in merry conversation with a gaggle of Railway Security Guards. He, too, boards the train home.

177

He sits, and sinks his hand into a plastic bag which advertises Silk Cut cigarettes. He brings out a camera, regards it with immense satisfaction.

It's been, all in all, a good day!

# A Crack At The
# Mirror

> In Bahrain once, the sahibs called the shots
> With many 'I'll be demmed's' and 'I say what's',
> The *Mirror* must retain its British tone
> And here's this Lankan who has dared to phone
> And seek a job—a job! He's got a brass!
> Let's get him here and kick his bleedin' ass!

There was that time when in Dubai that I developed an abiding hatred for a fellow named Zaffar. He was a sort of dogsbody for the *Gulf News*, and didn't like Sri Lankans. He was a sort of 'adviser' to our employee, Abu. A nondescript sort of fellow Zaffar liked to declare that he was a journalist in his own way and knew all about the breed. He was a smarmy little babu with badly cut hair and worse cut clothes and he resented us very much.

'We have the world's finest journalists in Karachi,' he used to say in a melancholy voice.

'Is that so?' I would say. 'They must have been trained in Colombo.'

Zaffar said he didn't like us and campaigned that we remain enforced bachelors. 'It's in your contract,' he reminded.

We were eloquently succinct. 'Bullshit!' we said, while G.W. Surendra scorned argument in English and would let loose a barrage of Sinhala in his characteristic sibilant growl which was a treat to listen to.

Usually, he would trace Zaffar to a semblance of early

man, somewhere between Ramapithecus and Homo Habilis and progress to explain why Zaffar had been taken off the human family tree and how he eventually came to the Arabian Gulf which, he insisted, was because of Zaffar's inherent urge to wallow in the dung of rutting camels.

And all because we had insisted on family accommodation and the opportunity to bring our families to Dubai.

But we won the day. Abu, with much weariness, introduced us to a fat Arab with a Lebanese moustache and a cheery smile. 'This,' he said, 'is Mr Ghazzi. He will obtain the visas for your wives and children. Give him all the details. You must fly them in at your own cost. I will provide you with the necessary furnished accommodation.'

Zaffar declared smugly that he may have lost a battle, but he hadn't lost the war.

'Do you know what I'd like to do?' I told Dudley Fernando.

'What?'

'Take Zaffar into some dark corner and whale the tar out of him.'

'This is not Sri Lanka,' Dudley objected. 'You'll be jailed and deported.'

'I suppose you're right. I really miss the simple, straightforward life.'

'Zaffar,' said Dudley gloomily, 'wants to see us zaffar.'

'Oh, damn your puns! I'm tired of this creep. Either he goes or I go!'

'Go? Go where?'

It was then that the idea germinated. 'Go to another newspaper. Abu can kill a goat to celebrate.'

182

'You cannot change your job,' Dudley said, 'not in Dubai anyway.'

'So I'll go to Bahrain or Kuwait or someplace.'

That night I telephoned the Dubai representative of the *Gulf Weekly Mirror*, a weekend tabloid that comes out of Bahrain. 'Do you need a sub-editor?' I asked him.

The representative, Alan Armstrong, asked: 'Are you British?'

'No.'

'Hum. I've seen your by-line in the *Gulf News*. You write reasonably well. Not tight enough for a tabloid. You use too many words. See me tomorrow. I'm watching TV now.'

'*Upstairs, Downstairs?*' I asked.

'Yes. Good series.'

'Yes,' I agreed, 'good British film with the servants downstairs and the pukka sahibs upstairs. I'll take the servants any day.'

'You're that kind of chap?'

'I don't know what you mean, but I'll see you tomorrow.'

I put the receiver down. Dudley looked up from his copy of *Middle East Economic Digest*. 'You'll never get the job. Englishmen don't like to be reminded of class distinctions. And anyway, how will you wriggle out of the *Gulf News* contract?'

That was a hurdle I would cross later.

Alan Armstrong was a nice fellow who suffered terribly from migraine. He tended to waffle somewhat when he got excited and within fifteen minutes of my meeting him, he was waffling. 'But you're a Sri Lankan,' he said, 'and Frown wants a Brit.'

Frown was Fallon Frown, editor of the *Mirror*.

Armstrong talked and I listened. The *Mirror*, he said,

was an exclusively British paper. There were Kennedys and Huttons and Wilsons and, of course, an Armstrong, but no Fernandos and Silvas and Lalchands. 'We do have a girl who is East European. Her name is Jadranka, but she's married to an Englishman named Porter, so that's all right.'

'Why don't you just get on the phone to Frown and tell him that you've got a Sri Lankan with the name of Muller. Tell him that perhaps I have ancestors who torpedoed all the British ships in the Channel and invaded the island of Guernsey.'

'You don't understand,' he said. 'We have a small team and we all work together in perfect understanding and harmony.'

'Meaning that I'll be a sort of nigger in the woodpile?'

'You don't understand,' he said again.

'Oh yes, I do. Why don't you let me talk to Frown? After all,' I added mischievously, 'he's hiring me, not you.'

'I told Alan to use his judgement,' Frown growled over the wire, on the offensive, 'you need not have disturbed me. I'm not trying to sound racist or anything. It's just that we are a newspaper run on true British lines.'

'You mean you have naked girls from Coney Island on page three?'

He snorted. 'Are you trying to be funny? I don't want a Sri Lankan sub-editor. There are Sri Lankans here, sweeping the street outside the Manama Centre where our office is. How can I hire a Sri Lankan? I have to think of the tone of the paper.'

I was ready to go up in flames. 'Do you know what the Arabs think about British journalists, Mister Frown? Have you read the anti-Arab stories recently in the *Daily Mirror* and the *Daily Mail*? And who are you? What are you really? You're just an Arab slave like the rest of us.

What tone are you speaking of? The tone of subservience? If you put a foot wrong you'll be on the next plane home. Just like me. And how many Brits are sweeping the streets in Saudi Arabia?'

'Look, Muller, let's not quarrel.'

'No,' I agreed. 'I'll come to Bahrain and punch your nose instead.'

'Listen,' he said wearily, 'I really need a good sub. Are you really Sri Lankan, with that name?'

'I am Sri Lankan,' I said, 'but if it's any consolation to you, everyone in my family is a British citizen. My parents live in Southend, and I've got five brothers and four sisters in England. I hope they are all living on the dole and diddling the economy of a tidy sum each week.'

'Put Armstrong on,' he said.

After three minutes Armstrong replaced the receiver and smiled. 'You're hired. When will you be ready to go to Bahrain?'

Blandly I informed Armstrong that my wife and family would join me there and that family accommodation was necessary. I also made sure that my letter of appointment included the clause that in event of termination, I would receive an air-ticket to Colombo. Armstrong did not stop to think. In the heat of the moment he gave me a most acceptable letter of appointment. The law says otherwise. An employee is entitled to an air-ticket back to the place he is employed from. Later, Frown swore mightily, like a modern Lars Porsena. 'I've been gypped,' he moaned. 'All I needed to do was give you a ticket back to Dubai!'

Dudley, my flatmate was the last to say goodbye. 'So you did it,' he said.

'Dudley,' I said, 'something has just struck me. We flew in here on the sixth of March. I fly today on the sixth of July. Fate seems to like knocking me for six.'

'Anyway,' he said, 'you have set a precedent. Keep in touch.'

Gulf Air served peanuts on the hour-long flight to Bahrain.

Looking down on the island, all I did see from three thousand feet, once we had swarmed through the cloud layer, was an immense plantation of date palms. From the air, Bahrain looks a small, cheerful place. 'How the devil do you land a Tri-Star here,' I wondered.

The runway seemed to peter out into the sea. Then, I reminded myself that the Concorde lands here and the Anglo-French combine has no suicidal tendencies. All said and done, there's much to be said for Bahrain's location, especially for aviators. In 1932, the first Imperial Airways plane landed here on its inaugural flight to India. Lots of pomp and pageantry. The Indian ambassador was said to have worn a diamond tie pin which made Arab dignitaries green with envy. At take-off, the plane sank into a disused water tunnel and had to be dragged out with ropes. Certainly not the thing one should think of when about to land!

The Concorde was on the apron. Its drooping face gives it that 'I've lost my mummy' kind of look and I've always had to fight the urge to take a handkerchief and go wipe its nose. Armed policemen at the foot of the gangway; armed policemen to chase you into the articulated bus; armed policemen to wave you into the terminal.

A little Indian looking like something out of Disneyland, with a red cocktail cigarette in his mouth, hailed me at the immigration counter.

'*Gulf Mirror!*' he announced, nodded when I raised my

hand and then called to the advancing group of passengers, '*Gulf Mirror, Gulf Mirror*, this way please . . . you are Mister Mullah? Good. I have your visa,' then turning to the mob in the arrivals area, '*Gulf Mirror*! Anybody *Gulf Mirror*?'

'Are you expecting others?' I asked.

'No, Miss Alison only give me your visa.'

'Then what the hell are you yelling *Gulf Mirror* at that lot? You're selling the paper?'

He grinned. 'Good to tell everybody coming here that have *Gulf Mirror* in Bahrain, no? I am Mister Gandhi. People call me Mister Fixit. I do immigration work. Residence visa, visit visa, re-entry permits, multiple re-entry, everything. Everybody in airport I know.'

Grabbing my passport he shoved it under the nose of a yellow-toothed Arab and let off a barrage of Urdu. The Arab punctuated this with glad cries of Arabic. It was all Greek to me. Snappily he chopped my passport. 'Valid for stay of one month unless residence permit granted.' Mr Fixit certainly knew his stuff.

'What about my unaccompanied baggage?' I asked him.

'Go to Bas,' Fixit said.

'Oh, is that Arabic for hell?'

He chuckled. 'That is Bahrain Airport Services. You are very right. Sometimes like hell.'

'Tell me, who is this Miss Alison?'

'She's Frown's secretary. Very uppy. She give you flat in building with other staff but put broken furniture. She say for Asians no harm broken furniture.'

I made a note. 'What about visas for my family?'

'Everything ready. You tell family to come. We go to airport to pick up.'

'Good.'

We climbed into the waiting car. On the dashboard was a sticker that read: LONG LIVE AYATOLLAH KHOMEINI.

Over a million people a year sweep into Bahrain, all looking for money, but many to relax between feverish bouts of moneymaking elsewhere in the Gulf. Bahrainis believe they are a cut above the rest. After all, they say, they have an archaeologically reputable history that goes back to the Palaeolithic Age of 50,000 BC. Ours is the original Garden of Eden, they claim with conviction. This land was Dilmun where, ancient texts say 'the raven never croaks'. In the airport arrivals lounge is a large three-dimensional map of the island which also refers to Dilmun and endorses the claim that this is the Garden of Eden.

Bahrain has other advantages. Unbroken Western influence has made the Bahraini a vastly more educated person than his Gulf brothers. But the oil is running out. The country is now a service centre and a big offshore banking centre for all those who want to diddle their respective countries out of legitimate taxes. And all the while, Bahrain wants to feel important. Surrounded, as she is, by other peoples' cash, there is this need to be as high spending and as modern as ever. At government level I met a pomposity that was ridiculous. The British, however, maintain that Bahrain is different.

'In what way?' I asked Chief Sub Ian Wilson.

'You don't need a permit to buy liquor,' he said, 'and you can chat up a Bahraini girl and nobody will throw you in the cooler.'

'Yes,' I admitted, 'that's different.'

I was swept into Fallan Frown's office. A podgy little man with the hint of a whisky nose. He made it clear that he had hired me out of dire necessity.

'That's OK,' I assured him. 'I accepted out of necessity. Do I get to work or do I see my flat?'

'Let me introduce you to Alison. She has made all arrangements.'

Alison gave me a Judas smile and simpered, 'Your appointment was a rush one and I didn't have time to furnish your flat adequately.'

'So you've given me discards and leftovers? Tell me, why do you wear your hair in a bun? You should wear it on your shoulders. You'll look really lovely then.'

In Sri Lanka if anybody had tried to sell me a broken chair, said body would have gone home with said chair wrapped around his neck. But I had learned a thing or two in the Gulf. Tell Alison that she has the potential to be another Siren of the Nile and she's on your side. Make love, not war. After all, this *was* the Arabic Garden of Eden.

The upshot was that she took all the rotten stuff away and fitted the flat with spanking new furniture, extra beds for the children, et cetera, et cetera.

'Tell me,' I asked, 'are Sri Lankans sweeping the streets outside this office?'

'No,' Alison said. 'There are some Indians who walk around with buckets of water and bundles of rags and offer to wash your car. All Public Works Department roadsweepers are Pakistani.'

I filed this away for further reference.

I also soon realized that the paper was one of the worst in the Gulf—a weekly which contained a hotch potch of rewritten stories from all manner of English-edited Gulf magazines and nothing dramatic or newsworthy whatsoever. One lolls around all week doing Fanny Adams because a sub-editor on the *Mirror* does not sub-edit. All he does is write headlines according to the type instructions given him by the Chief Sub. 'So this is the British way,' I said.

Wilson grinned. 'Simple, eh? I make all page layouts. I go through all copy and decide on its size, its spread and its position. All you do is give me the headline I want.'

After nineteen years in one newspaper or another in Sri Lanka I had never come up with such an idiotic procedure. One cannot exercise ingenuity or imagination.

'Look, I've got a peach of a headline for this story, but it won't go in two decks. Not with the type size you are specifying.'

Wilson would give me a pitying look. 'Too bad. Think of another headline.'

'You mean think of a headline you have already thought about when you gave me these type sizes?'

Wilson would shrug. 'If I can think of one, you certainly can.'

'Nothing doing. If you've got one, write it in and don't waste my time.'

We would stare at each other for long moments. 'You are being uncooperative.'

'No, I'm being sensible. What was your headline anyway?'

'I was thinking of something along the line of silk purses and sow's ears.'

'Good. That's really masterful.' The poor chap didn't stop to think. When the page proof went to Frown there was a minor explosion. Frown waddled out of his sanctum.

'Sow's ear! Sow's ear! In this Islamic country you talk of sow's ears? Good God!'

'So what?' I asked. As much as I didn't like Wilson, I liked Frown less. 'The commodities page gives prices for pork bellies.'

'Will none of you understand,' Frown would moan, 'pork bellies are commodities. They are in the market. We import pork here, and bacon and bangers and honey roast ham and franks and trotters and spare ribs and gammon—God! I'm hungry—but we don't put any pigs or hogs or sows in headlines!'

Wilson would scowl. He was particularly proud of that headline. Later he said to no one in particular, 'Frown should have called me to his bloody office instead of making a scene. After all, I'm the Chief Sub.' Why is it Chief Subs always think they are the Almighty?

'Cheer up,' I told him, 'make the sow a cow. Then you won't have to alter your typeface.'

'Cow's ear!' he yelled. 'You're batty!'

'Why not? Cows have ears.'

The look he gave me beggared description.

As one would imagine, the *Mirror* and I soon went our several ways. For one thing the *Gulf News* wanted me back. So did the *Khaleej Times* of Dubai and it was a toss up as to who would get me the visa first. The *Gulf News* won and I rejoined it as Supplements Editor. The *Mirror* folded. It had to. It was never meant to last, not with that marvellous 'tone'. But it's all filed under E for Experience. After all, it's the only thing—this Experience—that I may eventually carry to the cemetery!

*Comply And Complain*

I've come full circle—here's that cat again,
Remember how I said the creature could
Look on a queen and none would say it 'nay'?
Well . . . life, it seems is really not that good,
(Or maybe it was pissed on palace gin)
It staggered to the 'heads'; in sea of shit,
It gave a farewell yowl, and jumped right in!

A navy recruit does not take kindly to the menial work
that is thrust on him. He sniggers when he learns that
nautically, lavatories are called Heads. These navy types
are crazy. He also presumes that they are so called because
that is where the tails are flushed. But he bridles when told
that part of his many interesting duties is to scour the
heads. There is no use in telling duty officers that one
comes from a good family and one has never taken a mop
and bucket to scrub a lavatory. You are told, sweetly
enough, that this is part of a wrap-up training for
shipboard duty. On board, apparently, sailors clean
lavatories too. Someone, you are told, has to do it. So start
now. Get used to it. Yes, yes, I know, it's a load of shit, but
all life and living is, isn't it?

In the shore establishment HMCyS Rangalla where
we were trained, the lavatories were, in reality, massive
cesspits, dug deep beneath an awesome row of squatting
plates. This terrible place was christened Cigarette City
because, from days of yore, all recruits, forbidden to

smoke, had done so in the confines of the heads. It was a recruit haven. The heads and a cigarette . . . ah, bliss!

When a recruit is detailed to clean heads, an Able Seaman is also sent along to supervise operations. The Navy had apparently reasoned that a recruit on Heads Detail would smoke there if allowed to work unsupervised. It had never occured to the brass that smoking is usually done when a recruit is availing himself of the mod. cons., not cleaning them. I shrugged. I disliked this detail very much, and I didn't like the AB either.

'What's the use in you tagging along?' I told him. 'I can clean the heads without you.'

'You go and bring a bucket and squeegee,' he retorted. 'I'll do what I have to do and you do what you have to do.'

'So what have you got to do?'

'That's not your business. Go on!'

It was quite nauseating to find that one of the pits beneath a squatting plate held a dead cat. Able Seaman Jayasena looked at it interestedly and told me, 'Get it out.'

'What?'

'The cat. Can't leave a cat in the shithole. Get it out.'

I agreed. As it was, very large, green flies were buzzing over it, some even supping delicately. 'OK, I'll get a stick or something.'

Jayasena gave me a deadpan look. 'Just get it out now.'

'So all right. I'll get something to pull it out.

Jayasena spat. 'What stick? There are no sticks here. Take it out!'

'How?'

'With your fucking hand!'

I straightened up. Perhaps what the Navy had hoped to do from the 18th of November—discipline me—was now at that acid test stage, but I thought that this was pushing things too far. 'What? Put my hand in all that shit?'

'Yes! That's an order!'

The trouble with being a recruit is that every lowlife who has stopped being a recruit likes to give orders . . . and any recruit knows that he is in the cranberry sauce when someone yells, 'that's an order'. It means, in strict Naval parlance, that disobedience is tantamount to mutiny. In the old days, mutiny merited death or that unpleasant business of keelhauling, where the recalcitrant sailor is tied to a long line, tossed into the sea and dragged along the keel of the ship. The idea, then, is that a recruit must comply and complain. If I had wished to challenge this particularly unattractive AB's attitude, I had to (a) take the dead cat out of the pit with my hands, (b) complain to the Regulating Petty Officer, who would record my statement, (c) go before the Commanding Officer or First Lieutenant at a special Requestman's Parade to air my grievance and (d) abide by the C.O.'s or No. One's decision and judgement. (By the way, all First Lieutenants are known as Number Ones or Jimmys).

This sounds and seems most satisfactory. One feels that wherever one's ship sails, even halfway up Sri Lanka's central massif, the Geneva Convention is in operation and the rights of all mankind and naval recruits upheld and protected. What happens, of course, could well be something like this:

'Recruit Lal states that on the morning of November 28 he was ordered to bend over and grasp his ankles while Able Seaman Mendis and Able Seaman Ranjit swatted him on the posterior—'

'On the what?'

'Posterior, sir.'

'You mean his bum?'

'Yes, sir.'

'Then say bum, man.'

'Very good, sir.'

'Very well. Go on.'

'Yes, sir. Swatted him on the bum with a belaying pin. Recruit Lal states that he protested and asked why he was being so ill-used but he was told to shut up and bend over and that was an order. Recruit Lal complied and says he was hurt and humiliated. He says he received several blows on his post-um-bum. He now makes this complaint, sir.'

'Hmm. Is recruit Lal here?'

'Yessir. Ordinary Seaman Lal, two steps forward march!'

'Are the Able Seamen here?'

'Yes, sir.'

'Umm yes. Lal, you are very justified in making this complaint. You claim you have been assaulted. This is a serious charge. Have you any witnesses?'

'N-no, sir.'

'Oh, were you medically treated?'

'Sir?'

'Did you show your arse to the doctor?'

'No, sir.'

'Then what the devil are you wasting my time for? You! Mendis! Ranjit! Did you—'

'No, sir!' In chorus.

'There you are! Shall I tell you something, Lal? You come here rolling out some bloody bogus complaint to embarrass this camp and my position as Commanding Officer! DO YOU UNDERSTAND? You come here and waste my time and not an atom of proof! STOP FIDGETING! STAND ERECT!! Let me warn you, the next time you come before me I'll throw the bloody book at you. DID YOU HEAR?'

'Yer-yer-yes, sir.'

'Good! Now get out! Bum! Hah! Should have put the belaying pin up your bloody anus!'

It is thus seen that this comply and complain lark is a load of horse manure. I tried to reason with the AB. 'Surely you don't expect me to put my hand in that?'

'Yes. And hurry up!'

'But—'

'Look here. I won't tell you again. Get that cat out NOW! THAT'S AN ORDER!'

Well, put like that, there was no help to it. I leaned over, held my breath and plunged a hand into the mass of excreta. Once my fingers met that foul mess nothing else really mattered. I gripped a stiff, slimy leg and straightened up slowly. The cat dripped, stank fearsomely. Flies rose and were very indignant. My eyes were blazing. 'Here's your cat,' I hissed and swung it. It struck AB Jayasena on the chest, splattering muck on his face and neck. He howled, and then we both bolted for the taps, while he was squeezing shit out of his eyes, his boots scrunching on the dead animal that had a terrible face, all drawn back, fangs in a death snarl.

We soused each other, then skipped to our huts for soap and raced back to strip and lather each other. I, the thrower and he, the throwee had been liberally daubed because the soggy corpse had exploded against Jayasena's chest to spatter me as well. There was no time to start a fracas. We smelled. We reeked. Buck naked, we considered each other through swirls of lather and then our uniforms which lay wet, gunky, at our feet. In unison we kicked the clothes into the pit. 'Let some other bugger come and pull those out,' I said, and we scrubbed and scrubbed and soaped each other's backs and stood under the showers and laughed like lunatics. We left the bathroom, naked, sniffing at each other and the mountain wind raised goose pimples on us.

Jayasena said, 'Never brought a towel. What do I do?'

'Run like hell,' I advised.

'If somebody sees—'

'Can't be helped. My hut is closer. Run!' and two naked sailors dashed up the concrete steps, didn't check even to change gear, and flashing past an open-mouthed shipwright Fonseka, hurled ourselves into the hut.

Jayasena slapped me on the shoulder. 'I'll wear your towel and go to my hut and change.'

I was slipping into my trousers. 'No more dead cats, OK?'

He grinned. 'And no more shit in my face!'

It was better than an international summit!

# READ MORE IN PENGUIN

In every corner of the world, on every subject under the sun, Penguin represents quality and variety—the very best in publishing today.

For complete information about books available from Penguin—including Puffins, Penguin Classics and Arkana—and how to order them, write to us at the appropriate address below. Please note that for copyright reasons the selection of books varies from country to country.

**In India:** Please write to *Penguin Books India Pvt. Ltd. 11 Community Centre, Panchsheel Park, New Delhi 110017*

**In the United Kingdom:** Please write to *Dept JC, Penguin Books Ltd. Bath Road, Harmondsworth, West Drayton, Middlesex, UB7 ODA. UK*

**In the United States:** Please write to *Penguin Putnam Inc., 375 Hudson Street, New York, NY 10014*

**In Canada:** Please write to *Penguin Books Canada Ltd. 10 Alcorn Avenue, Suite 300, Toronto, Ontario M4V 3B2*

**In Australia:** Please write to *Penguin Books Australia Ltd. 487, Maroondah Highway, Ring Wood, Victoria 3134*

**In New Zealand:** Please write to *Penguin Books (NZ) Ltd. Private Bag, Takapuna, Auckland 9*

**In the Netherlands:** Please write to *Penguin Books Netherlands B.V., Keizersgracht 231 NL-1016 DV Amsterdom*

**In Germany :** Please write to *Penguin Books Deutschland GmbH, Metzlerstrasse 26, 60595 Frankfurt am Main, Germany*

**In Spain:** Please write. to *Penguin Books S.A., Bravo Murillo, 19-1'B, E-28015 Madrid, Spain*

**In Italy:** Please write to *Penguin Italia s.r.l., Via Felice Casati 20, I-20104 Milano*

**In France:** Please write to *Penguin France S.A., 17 rue Lejeune, F-31000 Toulouse*

**In Japan:** Please write to *Penguin Books Japan. Ishikiribashi Building, 2-5-4, Suido, Tokyo 112*

**In Greece:** Please write to *Penguin Hellas Ltd, dimocritou 3, GR-106 71 Athens*

**In South Africa:** Please write to *Longman Penguin Books Southern Africa (Pty) Ltd, Private Bag X08, Bertsham 2013*